Ripe for the Pickin'

{~}=#

Shana Thornton

Thorncraft Publishing
Clarksville, Tennessee

ISBN-13: 978-0-9979687-5-0
ISBN-10: 0-9979687-5-3

Cover Design by Erica Trout Creative
Author photo by Terry Morris

Library of Congress Control Number: 2021950997

Thorncraft Publishing
Clarksville, TN 37043
http://www.thorncraftpublishing.com
thorncraftpublishing@gmail.com

10 9 8 7 6 5 4 3 2 1

For Nana and Rita

About Book One, *Poke Sallet Queen and the Family Medicine Wheel* (2015):

When Robin Ballard takes a writing course in college, she goes searching for answers about her homeless father and wanders into the secret lives of her relatives as they gradually reveal their personal histories. Set in Nashville and the surrounding rural towns, *Poke Sallet Queen and the Family Medicine Wheel* offers a look into the superstitions and changes of a middle Tennessee family from the 1920s to the 21st century. Based on magic recipes, old journals, drunken revelries, midnight tales, some tall tales, and folk tales, Robin Ballard tells a "true" Tennessee family history.

The Family:
Robin Ballard – Narrator.
Daniel Ballard – Robin's father.
Miss Emy – Daniel's mother. Robin's grandmother.
Aunt Melinda Ballard – Daniel's sister. Robin's aunt who lives in Nashville and hosts Music City Mornings talk show.
Great Aunt Cora – Daughter of Hoot and Zona. Secretly the mother of Paul Ballard. Robin's great-grandmother.
Paul Ballard – Miss Emy's husband. Daniel's father. Robin's grandfather. (Deceased).
Hoot Ballard – Assumed to be Paul's father, but is actually his grandfather. Zona's husband. Cora's father. (Deceased).
Zona Ballard – Assumed to be Paul's mother, but is actually his grandmother. Cora's mother. (Deceased).
Nenny – Hoot's mother. Zona's mother-in-law. (Deceased).
Harold Flynn – Secretly the father of Paul Ballard.
Aunt Carolyn – Melinda and Daniel's sister. Robin's aunt.

The Band:
Robin Ballard – Vocals, Guitar, Mandolin.
Kevin Crenshaw – Fiddle and Vocals.
Angie Sparks – Fiddle and Vocals.
Martin Paxton – Bass and Vocals.

Ripe for the Pickin'

The Family Medicine Wheel Series
Book Two

{~}=#

Wild Roses

Medicine for long-awaited plans to fruit and long-kept secrets to be revealed

A fragrance across the fields,
A soft tempting
Delights in flower folds—
Smoothed.
Then, prick of thorn
To hint about the unknown
And draw blood from the depths.
A secret swells
High into the trees, climbing up and over
To tell—do tell—
Do linger across the blackberry,
Gazing over the old bramble and young saplings,
To weight the hips—
Scales heavy
With knowing pink
Blossoms in the sky.
Revelations
When they harden
Into orange, and rattle
A lighter load.

One | Opening Act

BELIEF DOESN'T LEAD to the future, and a faith in talents can't create life from imagination. No matter how much practice and development, our hands and feet are often choosing something else for us. Other peoples' stories push us onto unforeseen paths, too, since life forks out and, like the river, there are a multitude of side streams and little runoffs. I thought one course was the way to determine a future, and I learned quickly that once you start on a route, others open up into surprise vistas and sacred land, even formations in stone not so far away from the start. Mine sure did. I never thought my messing with a guitar out of boredom would lead to places I thought were just locations to play music. They also contained a connection to my family. I was on a track that I wouldn't have believed if someone had told me about it back in Granville when I was growing up.

No one was digging up the dirt anymore around the Ballard farm. It had long been settled other than under the steps of cattle. Of course, I had gone out there to find a treasure, I'm embarrassed to admit this cliché, following in a long line of other family members who also searched for a hidden trunk inspired by family legends. They looked amid hushed whispers or told everybody that they were the one who'd find it. I got in an argument with my grandma, Miss Emy, about it, as she saw it all as foolishness. She was fuming and waving that fan of hers at me.

My metal detector might have been beeping, but it blended right in with Aunt Melinda's car horn as she pulled up by the house. Miss Emy and I were both startled out of our reverie by the metal detector. Aunt Melinda came running and yelling. "Robin! Mama!" in a stream without taking a breath, but then thinking better of it, she yelled, "Miss Emy!" louder, having caught herself. I sensed her fear in ascribing Miss Emy a name she didn't say was okay. "Y'all out here?" she called hesitantly toward the medicine wheel. She paused long enough to listen for a breath and well up enough of hers to bellow out again, "Robin! Miss—"

"Over here!" Miss Emy shouted back, but Aunt Melinda carried on as if she hadn't heard her, though she paused and started up again at a closer range so that we knew she did hear her. "Miss Emy! Robin!"

"Would you hush?" Miss Emy yelled in the direction of my aunt.

"We're over here," I called out and picked up the metal detector, which lay atop lamb's ear and lemon balm and gave off a scent from touching it. The hydrangeas rattled a dry scratching against my arms. My aunt appeared beside Miss Emy who was on my heels and waved her fan in Aunt Melinda's face to show how annoyed she was by the disturbance and the shouting.

"What are you carrying on about anyway?" Miss Emy asked her daughter.

My aunt shooed her mother's fan away and clapped her hands together. "Robin," Aunt Melinda said excitedly. "I want to make you guess. I really do, but I'm just so excited that I don't know if I can." She bounced a little and clapped her hands together again. "Okay," she straightened her resolve. A serious look washed over her face. She even smoothed down the front of her shirt. Miss Emy looked amused, as if she might laugh at any moment.

"Guess," Aunt Melinda said to me.

"Guess what?" I asked.

"Just guess what I came to tell you," she said, trying not to smile.

"I have no idea, Aunt Melinda." I shrugged and looked to Miss Emy for a clue, but she arched an eyebrow and shook her head to the side. She flipped open her fan and began to flutter with amused glances back and forth between me and Aunt Melinda.

"Guess something," Aunt Melinda said. "Come on. You're no fun."

"What am I even supposed to guess?" I asked.

"Anything," she said, snapping her fingers. "That's the point."

"I don't know," I said. "You won the lottery?"

"No, no," she said. "Guess more."

"You got a new job?"

She shook her head.

"You bought a new car?"

"Nope."

"How can I possibly know this?" I asked. "This is too broad." My shoulders slumped, and I walked back over to the bench and set the metal detector on top of it. I was exhausted after being out there long enough for gnats to swarm my face as if the sweat was a puddle in the pasture. Miss Emy and Aunt Melinda followed behind me, talking away, as Miss Emy shooed the gnats and flies.

"You have to give a clue or something," Miss Emy said. "We could be here all night."

"You got a boyfriend?" I asked. Aunt Melinda smiled, and her face turned pink.

"Really? A boyfriend?" I asked and then realized that I sounded disappointed.

Aunt Melinda said, "Well, that's one of the surprises but not what I wanted you to guess." She smoothed her hair, and I noticed that she had a brassier color and styled it recently. Red highlights made her face look even rosier. I checked her clothes and shoes, noting that they were new as well. She was always stylish, but I could see by the details that she was a little fancier.

Miss Emy smiled at me and then Melinda. "A man?" she asked. "Who is he?"

"Just let Robin guess the surprise first," Aunt Melinda said, dismissing Miss Emy, who frowned and swatted her fan at a fly that buzzed loudly between us.

"Oh, you bought me a new car!" I was certain that this was it or something similar.

Then she said, "Yeah right, I already bought the car you have now," and she laughed at me. I must have wilted because she apologized and said, "Sorry to be so harsh."

I thought about the little two-seater hatchback parked in the driveway, and then I felt bad. I had been thrilled when she drove it over to me and told me that I could quit walking and biking everywhere. She had said, "You're graduating from taking the bus and begging for rides." I felt bad too for seeming ungrateful. "I'm sorry for assuming that you would buy another car for me. I'm thankful for it." My aunt waved her hand in my direction, signaling me to get on with her game.

"Now this is just making me depressed and doesn't seem like a good surprise," Miss Emy said and peered at my aunt with the same annoyance she trained on the fly. Whack! She hit the fly and knocked it down to the ground.

I looked at Miss Emy and said, "She's going to tell me that she planted me a garden of broccoli, isn't she? Maybe beets?"

Miss Emy chuckled. "A wild rose in your English rose garden," she said.

"Oh, you're not being very fun," Aunt Melinda said. "Fine, I'll tell you." She stopped short and suppressed a grin. "Well, are you sure that you won't try one more guess? I'll give you a clue like Miss Emy said. The surprise has something to do with your band."

"Poke Sallet Queen?" I asked. "The Family Medicine Wheel?"

She nodded with a wide smile as if she might have been on Music City Mornings right then. I even glanced around, over my shoulders, thinking that a cameraman might have followed her and be filming the whole thing. I listened, but only heard the gnats and flies, along with Miss Emy's fan making the teeniest whooshing breath between us.

"You got a big record deal for us?" I asked.

"No, but you might be able to work that out." She was giddy.

"You got them on your show, didn't you?" Miss Emy said, interrupting.

"Yes!" Aunt Melinda shouted and then turned and scolded, "Miss Emy! I didn't tell you to guess."

"Well, you were taking too long," Miss Emy said, and hit Aunt Melinda's arm with the fan.

Aunt Melinda waved her away, and said, "Robin, your band has an invitation to be on Music City Mornings with Melinda Ballard!" She started jumping up and down and bunny hopping in front of me. She squealed with glee. She gave me some of the details, how a band had canceled, how we were being offered their spot, and how we had to agree. She jumped more. It took a minute for it to sink in, but then I jumped with Miss Emy and her together in a little circle.

"I'm here for us to go celebrate," Aunt Melinda said. "I started to call and tell you, but that just didn't seem like the right thing to do. This feels bigger than that to me," she said. "And, I really wanted to tell you both about Gordon. I think he's in love with me, and I might have to marry him eventually. I know, Miss Emy. I know, Robin. It's shocking." I was certain that she had rehearsed all of this, especially after she answered my question, "How long have you been seeing Gordon," with "About two years."

"Two years!" Miss Emy slapped Aunt Melinda's arm again, but this time harder. "Shame on you. It's nasty of you not telling any of us."

"Is he married?" I asked.

"Or, was he married?" Miss Emy interrupted, "two or three years ago." She pursed her lips together.

"Not that it's any of y'all's business, but no, he wasn't married then and he's not married now. Not at least until he marries me." She rolled her eyes. "I can't believe you two."

"I'm sorry," I said, immediately feeling regret for misjudging her.

"I'm not," Miss Emy countered. "You're the one who keeps secrets and then thinks no one should suspect anything," she said to Aunt Melinda.

"Miss Emy, are you going to make me feel bad and argue with me or come with me and celebrate all of this good news?" she asked, urging us to follow her away from the medicine wheel.

"Is this Gordon with you?" I asked her suspiciously.

"No, he's not with me right now," she said, "but he might meet us out at the restaurant later."

"I need to get cleaned up," I said. "I don't feel so great. Plus, I kind of need to ask the rest of the band about the morning show before I celebrate being on it."

Aunt Melinda's face drooped. Her shoulders slumped a little. "I understand," she said trying to hide her disappointment. "Yeah," she said, "Of course you need to check with them first, but they'll say, 'yes.' They would be insane to let this go by."

"Go inside and call them now," Miss Emy demanded. "This isn't a time of mourning. This is great news. Call and tell them!" She waved me forward. "Go! Hurry up!" she said. She urged me on ahead of them. "They're going to be excited," she said. "Isn't this the kind of thing bands hope for?"

I started to run toward the house. "Thank you, Aunt Melinda," I called over my shoulder. I was smiling and breathless as I hopped up the stairs to the porch and put the metal detector down by the front door. The screen door clapped against the wood frame. I heard every sound. My feet as they made the hardwood floors creak and shift. My breath as it resounded back to me when I put my mouth up to the receiver. The buttons of the phone as I pressed them into the base of the phone. I dialed Kevin's number and was talking before I realized that I hadn't even looked for my cell phone to call him. Then, I remembered that it hardly ever got a signal out there anyway. My mind was making smarter decisions than my conscious awareness. I went straight for Miss Emy's old landline. I was a little foggy and felt as if I had receded from my body as I spoke into the phone.

"Kevin?" I asked, even though I knew it was him. Everything seemed so clear but confusing at the same time, as if I couldn't quite believe that I had arrived at the moment in the way that I had gotten there. If I hadn't gone for Miss Emy's landline automatically, then I wouldn't have realized, as I did in that moment, that I had Kevin's phone number memorized, that I called him first and dialed the digits, and that our band was going to have a spot on a Nashville morning show. I had never even considered taking the band on the show or asking any favors of Aunt Melinda.

"Your aunt is who?" Kevin asked. "Is this a joke?" he asked after I confirmed the third or fourth time that my aunt was the morning show host he had watched while growing up and while getting ready to go to work as an adult.

"I have to sit down," he said after a long pause. "I love you," he said and then laughed.

"What?" I asked. At first, my head was dizzy until I realized that he was saying "I love you" in reference to my aunt getting our band a spot on the show, not because he was confessing his love for me, as I had suddenly felt overwhelmingly in love with him. Yet, I had to wonder if he had reciprocal feelings for me, though I didn't think our feelings matched exactly and I wasn't sure how they were mismatched either. Certainly, we had chemistry from our first meeting. Maybe it was fear inside Kevin that stopped him from asking me out, or maybe our spark simply didn't have enough fire to create passion. I wasn't going to risk our friendship or our band in order to find out either. Sometimes, there was no going back to singing along together and jamming out in a band if someone reveals that they have a crush. I knew to wait and find out if things changed in the future.

In the meantime, Kevin said, "I can answer for everyone in the band with an emphatic, 'Hell, yes!' to being on Music City Mornings!"

He let out a "Woo! Yeah!" and I had to hold the phone away from my ear until his celebratory shouts died down. "Oh, wait," he said. "When are we supposed to be on the show? How long do we have to prepare?"

"They had a cancelation," I said. "That's why we're on in the first place. We've got to take it even though it's next week. If we say, 'no,' then we're saying, 'no,' for good."

"Then, we're saying, 'yes.'"

Kevin offered to call Angie and Martin to give them the good news, since I didn't know where I had placed my cell phone before I went to the fields looking for the treasure.

"Thank God your aunt got this gig," Kevin said before we hung up. "I was getting worried about you turning into a crazy person in search of buried treasure. It's good to finally hear from you. Hell, yes!" He shouted out again excitedly. I could almost hear his grin coming through the phone receiver. "I've been waiting for this for a long time, Robin Ballard, so thank you!" I knew that he was standing in a circle of sunlight somewhere.

It was one of those phone calls that cause you to walk outside and say, "What did you just say?" One of those calls that transforms into a smile. We made a plan to meet the next day for a rehearsal.

I opened my songwriting notebook, and started drafting a new song.

Opening Act
Lyrics by Robin Ballard

Even if we didn't stay together for the long road,
You were a solid opening act.
You got me on the right track.
I was playing and singing without looking back.
We jumped up on our stage
And we owned it, we owned it, without looking back.

You said let's go out on the road

Let's show them what we've got—
This solid opening act
Always on the right track.
I tried to warn you that we were missing something
I lost the energy when I tried to sing
I couldn't make it happen
Couldn't bring it back
To our solid opening act
And get on the right track again...

Violets

Medicine for finding young love, fresh and delightful,
surprising and sweet, but beware, it could wither in the heat

Freckled in early spring
And speckled suddenly in snow,
Those blue eyes shine and reflect
The lilac and purple sunset glow.
A fresh love, edible candy.
Treats leading us into a search.
We seek soft sandy
Rain, soggy violets perch
In clover
Falling over.

Two | Dress Rehearsal Times

"I WANT YOU to try this," I said to Kevin and Angie, offering them both a cup of tea. "Tell me if you like it."

She sniffed the drink. "It smells green," she said. She sipped. "Sweet grass, slightly flowery." I motioned for her to hurry up and try another sip, but she enjoyed trying to guess what it was before tasting it again.

"Good," Kevin said. "Mmmm, really good." Kevin went on to start our practice before we had a chance to talk about the violet tea, though I asked, "Would you believe that I picked them in the backyard this spring and dried them?"

Kevin wrote the words, "Backyard Spring" into my songwriting journal, and we continued with the practice. We had a lot to discuss, so I didn't take up the time talking about tea. We were all in agreement, so I strummed and picked until my little fingertips were numb in knowing the songs. On Music City Mornings, they were giving us the time to play two numbers and we might get to talk for two minutes, too. Plenty of twos to go around, and those took us that far, onto the show, which was a flash in the pan looking back at it all, but we had one singular problem.

In my arrangements of music, it was an issue that we needed to solve if we wanted to play some bluegrass songs. We needed a banjo player. In a town of all the genres of Americana, bluegrass and folk, not to mention country, we fit in just fine with two fiddlers who could also sing. Both Kevin and Angie had that covered. Then, there was me on guitar, mandolin, and main vocals, and Martin on standup bass which definitely served as our beat plenty of times. He could play the banjo, too, but he didn't have any love for it. When I pressed him, he fled even more. Kevin warned me that I was driving him away.

We were creative and, dare I say, innovative at times, in our arrangements. I even played a dulcimer every now and again, and I felt that there was something complete in most of our songs, even if it couldn't be that way from a bluegrass point of view. So, I still wanted that banjo for some songs, and I was pressing them to experiment here and there. You might say that I even whined and begged when we first started practicing together. No one could find a banjo player that we wanted to invite to practice with us. Even I was particular. By the time Aunt Melinda gave us the morning show opportunity, I yearned silently for balance on some songs that I knew we needed. I didn't want to overemphasize fiddling until we got stuck in the never-bet-the-Devil-your-head style. I was itching to get a banjo player.

The passage of time was fluid as fingers on strings in harmony, and we naturally moved onto Music City Mornings as if we performed it every morning. We joked for two minutes with Aunt Melinda and hit every note on cue.

Angie read from the newspaper review. "The viewers loved that Nashville hometown feel, where they got to meet Melinda's niece after all these years. Listening to her sing was a bonus. That's a voice we definitely want to claim as one of Nashville's own." Angie looked at me over the paper. "What a write-up!" She sighed. "Let me read you what they wrote about me." She pointed a curl with her fingertips. It swooped around her cheek.

"I'm listening," I said.

"Yeah, that's it," she smirked. "I'm not the queen. You are."

"There's nothing about the rest of the band?" I was stumped.

"Honey, we're your royal subjects," she said tartly. "I'm kidding," she said after I sulked. She cleared her throat, "The Family Medicine Wheel, her band, could easily steal the show with their eclectic appearances and harmonies, but instead they complement Robin's unique voice with their own remarkable blend of sounds."

I breathed and closed my eyes for a moment in a smile. I pictured us, as I had many times before, but this time I tried to truly see and hear us through the eyes of strangers.

Kevin usually wore jeans when he wasn't working as a nurse. He was tall and had a presence on the stage, the main guy, you might say. He wore a button-down shirt, sleeves rolled up to the elbows. His Predators ball caps rotated with a couple of others, but I knew that he had a lucky Preds' one. He sported a different pair of cowboy boots all the time. I teased that he must have a dang room full of boots, but he assured me they all fit in his closet. I knew that they were stacked "plumb up to the ceiling," I joked him as Miss Emy would have. He was a big guy, commanding on stage, but he didn't have a gut or anything. He was solid, and he'd chosen a typical pointed toe pair of black boots for the morning show. He looked sharp on the stage, even though he was wearing a ball cap.

"I bet he could make a tuxedo look good with a ball cap sitting on top," Aunt Melinda elbowed me back stage before we went on that morning. I rolled my eyes at her. She took off after him to talk about who knows what. I cringed and tried not to notice the butterflies that emerged in my stomach before we went on the show and then when I was remembering it while talking to Angie later.

Angie was a great complement to everyone on the stage. She had a ballerina's ability to move gracefully on the stage and play with Kevin and Martin *and* me. Her hair, her pixie-like energy, gave the Celtic impression of a modern-day fairy. She wore all kinds of different clothes—sometimes a flowing dress, thin and filmy, and other times she wore tight jeans and a t-shirt. That morning, she was in the flowing dress, a deep brown one.

Martin also wore a button-up shirt and jeans for almost every performance, except when it was too hot and he opted for a t-shirt. He wore craft beer shirts that he collected. He fixed his wavy auburn hair in the mirror before we went on stage. He carried a mirror in his backpack for that purpose. He wore Chuck Taylors, different colors. They were huge, his feet, because he was tall and skinny. He was one of those people who seemed to open up more and more as he stood, as if folded apart. You didn't think that he could keep getting taller as he stood. Someone as short as me couldn't believe it. He matched the stand-up bass. They belonged together and made a dramatic appearance on stage when he played alone for his recitals. Because we were both in school together, I was usually the one from the band to attend his university performances. He was on his way to becoming a virtuoso, and I worried that his classical training would eventually lure him away from us.

I always hoped that I looked that good with my guitar on the stage. I liked wearing little dresses in the summer, but Angie begged me to change my appearance for the stage. I wasn't going to budge until she pointed out how many people were wearing sun dresses and cowgirl boots...with jean jackets. I rolled my eyes at her and conceded, "Alright, you're right. It's too typical sometimes." I looked down at the pile of clothes we'd been going through and sighed irritably. "What am I supposed to do? Buy all new clothes? I can't do that."

"Why don't you wear dresses similar to mine?" she asked wincing, thinking that I wouldn't like the idea. I gave a nod and said that sometimes it'd be okay with me. "I could let you have some. I have one with an opening at the leg that would be so pretty on you. It's like this deep purple and a 1940s style meets a mariachi band." She jumped up and down, proud of herself. "That's it!" she declared.

I wasn't convinced, and consulted Aunt Melinda the day before we were supposed to go on Music City Mornings. She led me to her closet and pulled out a bunch of pairs of bell bottoms and some lace shirts.

"Mix it up," she said. "Sometimes, wear the dresses and jean jackets. Other times, the long flowing look, but for the show tomorrow, put on a pair of bell bottoms, like these." She held up a hip hugger pair of soft, pale denim and slight bells. She had a black lace shirt that made a perfect contrast, "showing that flat tummy just a little," she winked. I wore that outfit on the show, long black hair, black wedges, and my guitar with my favorite guitar strap. It had a beaded pattern that was made on a loom. I got it in a little shop where we played one night. The woman was stringing it right there during our show. She gave it to me afterward.

I enjoyed my varied style, and I would just as likely wear my boots and a dress as I would a tank top, big elephant bell jeans, and a cowgirl hat with a pair of flip flops. I even went barefoot sometimes. I loved my woven cowgirl hat, and I wore it a lot. I dressed up sometimes, too, in fancier flounces, depending on the venue. I was *not* about to start being confined.

Even though we didn't go on the show the day it actually aired on TV, we still filmed it in front of a live audience. That part of it felt like going out to do any other gig. Every one of us had our own superstitions before we performed. It's funny how a lot of that has to do with what you look like, some part of our appearance, but that's the thing that we can control about the show. So, that's why we focus on it like it makes some kind of magic or brings some kind of luck. All of the hype about the show inspired my songwriting notebook to fill up with partial songs and ideas.

Dress Rehearsal Times
Lyrics by Robin Ballard

I pulled that little lucky dress
Out of the drawer in my hand-me-down chest.
I stood in front of the mirror
Just wishing that I was luckier, maybe flashier.
Would they laugh at me?
Would they scoff at me?
Would they send me off the stage sayin', "Next."
I was embarrassed by that hand-me-down dress,
Thinking about it more than doin' my best.

Stuck in dress rehearsal times.
Stuck in dress rehearsal times.
Take two on dress rehearsal times.

Would they even see or hear the real me
Beyond these dress rehearsal times?
So, I tried on a luckier dress
And, I thought I had the best
But I stumbled and I fell
There was no way I was gonna sell
Something other than myself
In my old lucky dress
From my hand-me-down family chest.

I'd get out of the dress rehearsal times
By being true to what's mine
My songs, my hair, my shoes, my dress
This lucky hand-me-down dress....

"'This little treasure of a band is sure to surprise us in the future, Nashville. Make sure you check out their next shows.'" Angie paused in her reading of the newspaper. "And they list our next four shows," she said.

"That's good," I said, again relieved that she had been teasing me earlier and not serious.

"It's a wonderful review," she said. "Beyond good. We're lucky." She fanned herself with the newspaper. Before Angie read the rest of the review, I was afraid that we had entered one of the most typical issues in a band—that the rest of them secretly thought that I was getting all the attention and not giving them their due credit.

I was prepared to defend myself and had created a speech to prove that I had acted in ways that lessened those typical band issues. I always introduced everyone in the band and told a little story about them. They all had solo moments and singing moments, and anything else they wanted. Songwriting credits, choreography say-so, and ideas they wanted to try out. I was prepared to tell any of them that I didn't control the band and didn't want to, but I never had to say any of this. They weren't concerned about it. Everyone was trying to be fair. It was unusual, as we learned on our journey, to be a band that got along so well. People made bands out of their families and went out on the road in big tour buses and couldn't stop arguing. Husbands and wives commanded that buses stop in the middle of a Tennessee highway and let one of them off. Best friends picked fights and got back-up singers to spread rumors about the other one in the duet. It went on and on.

Instead, I sat in the backyard, drinking my violet tea over ice from a mason jar, and asking, "How did you know that this would be so good cold?"

Kevin shrugged. "Same way it's so good hot." He giggled. "I always add a little vodka or whiskey to mine," he whispered, though no one was around except me.

"I like the cold version."

He nodded. "Didn't you tell me that you picked the violets from the backyard this spring?"

"Yeah," I said. "Pretty cool, huh?" I gazed out, imagining the little purple faces of the violets. "You wrote it as a song title in my journal, Backyard Spring, but we never made a song out of it.

"Well, damn, we need to do that," he said taken aback. "It's not like me to forget a song like that."

"Think of all that's happened since then," I said. "I'm gonna start writing it now, though. We can't let it go again."

"Yeah, it's like someone cast a magic spell on us. As if your Aunt Melinda is our fairy godmother," he said.

I turned to him, surprised, "I can't believe you just said that. I've thought that since I was a kid," I said.

He looked down at his tea as if the answer arrived from there. He swirled the mason jar. "But you know, I keep wondering, who's gonna try to stop us? Take our tickets and attend the ball without us?" He winked into his drink and gulped it down.

Backyard Spring
Lyrics by Kevin Crenshaw and Robin Ballard

I over-thought so many things
Let all these worries linger in my brain—
I imagined all that I
Thought you wanted me to do.

Imagined another town,
Imagined a ball gown,
Imagined some other shoes
Too fancy for me to say I do.
Keepin' it simple
Doesn't come easy
In that fast glamour world.
I want nothing more
Than to make you proud
And to stop this constant whirl
Stop
And feel the cool dew on the grass
I'm kneeling for you
In the backyard spring
Asking if you want me too.
Quite simply,
So simply,
I want you, I do.
And I'm kneeling for you
In this backyard spring...

Elderberries

Medicine for the sun's energy for work, each part of the process leading to completion

Shake and Catch,
Boil and sift,
Strain and mix,
Blend and sip
The work of elders
Beneath the trees.
The bark: Grind. The fruit: Simmer.
Cold glass jars.
Cinnamon and cloves.
A dark, purple punch.
A pucker with honey.
Drink me round with the sun's route.
A call from the watcher
"Time to gather the berries."
Process, the repetition of medicine.
Repel illness. Bless vitality.

Three | Lyrics & Tonics

I WAS SPENDING much of my time writing—both songwriting and the next stage of my family project. I often sat with Aunt Cora, writing down her recipes and anything else she wanted to tell me. I envisioned those old family remedies and recipes as a book that I could give as a gift to her and Aunt Melinda. Secretly, I kept pondering the idea that a recipe book would be a great fundraiser for the homeless shelter and food kitchen where my dad worked. I hadn't told him yet, but the idea brewed in me like a good song builds from melody to lyric to finding someone who harmonizes with me and works out all the details where my inspiration left off.

Since I thought it was important to try out the recipes first hand, Miss Emy helped me by foraging for herbs on the farm and drying them. I drove out there and helped collect some of them, though Miss Emy did most of the work.

It also gave me plenty to talk to folks about when we were finished playing music and sitting around at a bar. I started writing down the recommendations of people who came into our regular hangout, Love's Rest, a historically famous restaurant just outside of Nashville, and where plenty of tourists still visited and wanted to hear some authentic music.

Angie's friend managed the place and let us play there every other Saturday afternoon. That gave us the chance to try out our new songs on an audience and to practice interacting. Playing Love's Rest couldn't have been better for our band, and the regulars began to follow us, too, and were becoming our fans.

Martin's dad lent us a minivan and we hit most of the bordering counties. There were little festivals to play. I was amazed that the more I talked about plants, the more people shared their family remedies. It was easy to start the conversation. All I had to do was say "elderberry." That one plant was like saying, "Abracadabra" or "Open, Sesame" or any other magic spell. Soon, a whole table full of people was gathered around me after a show at a bar or restaurant, telling me about their Granny's famous elderberry syrup or home remedy.

My family kept a jar of it in the fridge. The mason jar was ringed by the stain. The smell was cinnamon and cloves escaping from the glass of cold berry juice. I recalled the process, when my aunts would arrive to help Miss Emy every year. She swore that it was something Hoot and Zona started. She said the tincture saved us all from the cold and the flu so not to argue about it and just help. We all pitched in. Shaking the trees on a far field, carrying blankets of berries and pouring them into buckets. Boiling and straining. Mixing and blending.

The aunts believed in it as a preventative. Aunt Carolyn gave spoonfuls to each child while they were growing up. Miss Emy got mad because Aunt Carolyn always took extra jars for her sister-in-law. She even tried to sneak it out to her car when she thought no one was paying attention. The tonic was that powerful, and everyone wanted to scare the cold. Miss Emy froze a bunch of berries, so occasionally in the winter, I helped with new batches—filling canning jars, labeling them with dates, stacking them down in the cellar. Miss Emy walked out over the fields every summer, and when she thought the berries were about to ripen, she called Carolyn to plan for the annual event. Miss Emy reminded her, and everyone else, "Your Ma Zona said, 'Medicine is a process,' and she was right about that."

I loved hearing about the recipes and remedies that people had stacked in cellars and on shelves. On the road, when I talked to people about herbs and remedies, after elderberry syrup or wine, or a tisane, people named honeysuckle wine and chickweed salve. I listed things by county, just to keep up with the differing recipes and varieties of herbs and native wild plants for each one. When we got the call for an Atlanta festival, I was equally excited for the gig as I was about talking to folks about plant lore. It offered access to a lot of people.

To prepare for the festival, we decided to meet and make plans for Kevin's absences caused by his nursing schedule. No one wanted to find a replacement, but we also didn't want to stop being a band or accepting jobs to fit Kevin into all the plans. We performed better with him. I was so agitated that I couldn't write any new music.

After that meeting, he called me one afternoon and asked if I'd ride with him the next morning to work on songwriting somewhere special. When I

asked *where*, he said, "A park about two hours away."
Then, "Bring your great-grandpa's notebooks, too."

In the dark of early morning, we rode in silence
and watched the patterns of light change as we wound
with the fog through the forest. Daybreak on the quiet
roads helped me to settle. I carried a mandolin, and it
served as our music for the drive with Kevin
sometimes humming. The morning was bright but not
many vehicles were in the parking area. Kevin
retrieved his fiddle, and I followed him on a path
through the woods to a cliff overlooking a stone
opening in the bluff, where Kevin sat and played his
fiddle. A big chunk of rock jutted out over the valley
below. The rock contained fissures and openings,
slices overlooking the treetops.

I walked down the opening, stairs that had been
cut long ago into the stones, some narrow and others
uneven and wider on one side. I left Kevin at the top.
As I descended, the stone walls rose taller and taller
on either side of me, and I passed small trees and little
banks of dirt and moss. The rock changed, different
shades of gray, but so many more colors than that,
and the rich texture swirled it together with shimmer.
When I reached the sunlit bottom and exited the
stone passageway, the valley of the South Cumberland
lay before me, and chills covered my arms as the wind
blew. Looking back up the stone stairs, I thought of all
the people who moved through this passage.

Kevin's music drifted, and I hurried back up to
him, feeling the verses welling up inside my fingers
and throat. We sang above the cleft in the stone and
wrote songs carried by the vultures over the valley.

He flipped through Hoot's notebook and chose a line, singing it to me like a question: "She reflects the colors of flowers," to see if I approved. I nodded and improvised. The pages flapped in the wind imitating the wing beats of the big birds. I weighed the pages down with rocks. Our knees touched and shards of stone dug into my legs after sitting and playing for so long that eventually my leg rested on top of his and he wasn't playing his fiddle anymore, only singing and humming. I wanted to know how it would feel to sleep there under the stars with our music playing and a fire glowing above the treetops. I sent the desire out floating across the valley as we drove back and he dropped me off to the blaring sound of my neighbor's car alarm.

I wrote the makings of three new songs the next day. I wasn't even finished reading Hoot's journals. I had read parts of the one I took with us a few times, but it was more than looking for secrets now. Some favorite passages inspired songwriting for all of us, and were helping us write for the new album.

I liked the feel of this book's soft leather cover and the flap that folded across the front of it. The leather was tan and scratched up from the years of being passed around and hidden away. A few ink marks were on it and the ring from a wet cup was sealed into the back of it. It was the book that had the pages torn out of it that Cora gave to me long ago.

Most of the notebooks were actually hardback books bound in cloth. One of them was dark blue and the paper was so thin I could see through it. *Bible paper*, I thought. *Sacred paper* was my next thought. I couldn't read much of what was written in it. The pages were yellowed, the ink or pencil faded almost to transparency with other places where something had spilled or smeared the ink. There were even some pages stuck together in a wad with glue or flattened gum or something. I wanted this one to be my new favorite. I hadn't pored over the pages yet since I knew it was a mess from my first perusals, but each time I picked it up, I felt a swell, a surging and cooling against my fingertips. I also sensed a rush of energy when I imagined going to play a lot of paid gigs.

I looked at the black-covered journal with the missing front cover. The spine and back cover of the book were fine. A few threads hung from the spine where the cover had been ripped off of it, but the spine was still solid and hadn't splintered anywhere. The black was dull and smooth on the back cover, and I carried it as if the back was the front, and I always flipped it over after opening it. This is the journal that Angie liked so much when we were songwriting and sometimes I had fun slapping her hand so that she would leave it alone.

"I just like looking at how this dude wrote," she said. "Hoot was so Renaissance." She raised an eyebrow. "So ahead of his time. He would be one of those yuppie farmer brewery owners now. It's a big trend out west. My aunt owns one in California that's a winery farm thing." She threw up her hands as if the concept confused her or maybe she wondered why she didn't own one herself.

"You're right. Hoot would want a farm restaurant and brewery for sure."

From Hoot Ballard's Journal, the one with the soft leather cover:

June 2, 1960

Miss Emy is formal. She flutters a fan. I don't know where she picked it up. I want to help her, but she resists interference. When I watch her, I want to tell Paul that he ought to have loved her better'n he did. She's smart as any other woman who grew up on a farm and knows the ways of animal and plant and mystery, but she is more fulfilled by the city's turn of events, the lights and steel, the commotion of doing with cars, trains, and stores. Yesterday, she called me "a hero," and not a soul has ever said that to me. We are more similar than different.

I am the one who loves Zona with passion and deliberation, understanding her wisdom even as I am confounded by her belief in manipulative practices. My soul yearns to understand the interworkings of mystery and life's cause, yet I will walk toward a light of dignity and a truth that is possible. I do witness my own hypocrisy as evidenced by my disregard for honesty and law. Though if the laws of this land had been fair and just, if commerce were open to all, my contributions would surpass the means needed for me to stay safe with lies in order to conduct my business.

June 18, 1960

I pinch back the thyme to make more. It offers a profusion of sprawl on the hot stones. Nothing daunts it, even when I pinch it.

Dandelion faces in the early fields are soft. I swirl my thumb into the flower. Pull back the sides and press the softness forward, tracing it against my cheek.

That honeysuckle tincture improves my mood. The overwhelming effusion of the fragrance envelops me, and I am cast underneath it without being able to see out, as if under a weeping willow, the smell dripping an invisible umbrella all around me like a lid to keep it in my nose and my body. A lightness moves through me, reaching up and out with flickering pink pulses just as the stamens of the flowers spider out into the sun.

July 23, 1963
Melinda is pure delight. She reflects the colors of flowers. She plants and sings. Miss Emy wants to hold onto the girls and keep them over there, but they love it here. Carolyn says that she'll live with us one day, and she was born with the way to see forward. It will be so. Carolyn will follow her sister until she doesn't anymore. Melinda will want to be the overseer one day, the one to tell them all how to live. The Angels around them shine the truth of their futures in almost every moment of their lives that I witness. They each have an Angel, always around. When I pray, I ask them to stay with the children in our family. When I pray, I ask for an Angel to bless me with presence and forgiveness. When I pray, I ask the Angel to speak on my behalf to the Almighty and give us the clarity to see the beauty of this place and reach out to Her People in Love. Amen.

~ ~ ~

This passage was one of my favorites. I was using the one about honeysuckle to write a new song. It struck me that Hoot wrote about the spiritual with universal language and imagery at times. The last sentence pointed straight into my heart every time.

The way he used the word *Her* and capitalized the H. I questioned, *Did he intend that? Was it a mistake?*

And, I wanted to doubt it at first, but he wrote an undeniable "Her" instead of "His." Whether it was deliberate or a slip, I was fulfilled when I first read it. These were the types of things I was looking for when I collected his journals in the first place. Yes, I had wanted to find out if he would reveal family secrets within them, and he sort of did. More than that, once I got a little hint of these other types of revelations within the journals I was searching for those now. I didn't even know I longed for this connection with my great-great-grandfather when I started gathering the stories, and even when I was chasing them down more intently. This spiritual connection was one of the sweetest rewards for following through on the whole project.

Truthfully, each sentence I read made me more and more certain that a spiritual current was guiding my life. That's why I couldn't leave them all behind anywhere, and I was carrying one of them with me all the time. Even Martin wanted to use them, saying after we tried and tried to come up with a line for a song that we were writing and hoping to try out soon, "Come on and just open up one of them magic books of your great-granddaddy's and let's use a line."

Lying there, I opened a new one and read a passage. This journal was a faded, dark green hardcover. The journals were all quite small by comparison to today's standards. They measured about the size of my palm. The green one had a loose spine that wiggled more than it should when I opened it. A pocket of air puffed along the length of the spine, so I knew it had separated from its binding. The tan pages were thicker than the previous journals I read. The ink was perfect and shone out in rich contrast to the paper. I hadn't noticed that it was in such good condition because I had been so focused on inspecting the other journals.

The smell reminded me of being lost in the big old closets in Miss Emy's house. I'd never imagined Hoot walking through the house until then. I'd never imagined how they lived in there without toilets and with a detached kitchen, too. No running water, and then adding the plumbing, the pipes, sinks, toilets. That was all Hoot and whichever sons he had convinced to help him. Coal. Wood fires. Electric fans. Later, air conditioning units in the windows. The house had seen transformation again and again. I marveled at how they must have constantly worked to conceal the past within those changes for improvement and modernization.

The smell of the house is what revealed its age to me more than anything else. In the attic, the closets, the drawers, the canning cellar, that's where I wandered sometimes over the years, where I'd find a random instrument, the mandolin and dulcimer, or an old magazine, a dust-covered fan that Miss Emy abandoned somewhere, old clothes and tablecloths, doilies, and needlepoint, recipe books, coupons, and catalogues. They all held onto that smell of aging, a time when this book was penned, which held this fragrance of aging and other human interests and eras.

Hoot Ballard's green journal:

December 24, 1952

The family gathered around the fire and we sang for hours this afternoon and into the evening. We turned on the lamps. Zona and Jane lit the candles. I missed Cora and Dalton, wishing they would have changed their minds about staying in Nashville for this Christmas. I half expected to see their car arrive and for her to declare that she couldn't miss seeing the whole family all together. All my boys and their families, the grandkids, all arrived for an evening to plan ahead for the future, rejoice in our shared blessings given by the Providence of Heaven, and clasp our hands together whilst raising voices in song. We played the instruments and made a merry music. Cousin Garnett brought his daughter Elizabeth and her family, but Cora wouldn't be persuaded even with this knowledge. Zona told her that the house was equipped to hold everyone.

Old Man Gibbs is putting up some of the family at his house. He was here for the first hour of our gathering. I noticed that when Zona and the women got to talking and prophesying, he wished everyone a Merry Christmas and walked home. The rest of the group going there stayed here until about midnight and they all piled into Jane's car, sitting on top of one another, and drove over there.

I walked around after everyone either left or fell asleep. The moon is nearly full, and this year it is a mite warmer than usual. I walked down to the hollow and spring. Steam rose up toward the moon. I slipped my shoes off and sat down on the stone. It was cold until my feet were in the warmth of the pool.

Looking at the moon in the water there, I said to it, "Almighty, if there's a way you can hear me, and you can protect this family I've grown here, please let me know.' The owl sounded out that call for my name just after I said it. I turned and couldn't see the owl, even though it sounded close behind me. I felt the sensation of the mystery wash over me, and I thought of my Ma teaching me how to ask the Almighty to talk to me and the Almighty will speak if we listen. She said the Almighty likes to be heard.

~   ~   ~

I put down the journal and picked up my guitar, slid it across my belly and stayed mostly reclined. Even if it looked awkward, the weight of the guitar was comfortable. I played lightly, looking up at the ceiling with my eyes closed for a long time. I liked feeling the motion of the music, the resonance, without my eyes being open. I had fallen asleep like that many times, and the sliding of the guitar off onto the floor woke me. I often couldn't sleep well, and I played long into the morning, but by the time the sun came through the windows, I was hugged around my guitar and the notebooks, asleep.

When songwriting begins to coalesce for an album, it develops energy. I often heard about it. Even in class, we learned about bands and composers locking themselves away when they're on a writing spree. I trembled just a little in my fingertips because I was pretty sure that it was happening for me. No matter whether or not people liked our album, we were writing one—our own.

Kevin and I kept the momentum going. Not too long after that first drive, Kevin asked if I wanted to go to a similar place. On the drive before dawn, I asked, "What made you want to do this? Go out to these places and play music?"

He shrugged and blushed. "I just thought it would be different. I also still want to matter to the band, and I like songwriting."

"How did you think of it?"

"Just wanted to do something with you," he said. "Unique." He adjusted his cap nervously. "My parents used to take our family to parks and battlefields all the time. It might seem kind of boring to most people, but I always thought it was interesting." He shrugged. "It just popped in my head, and I kept imagining playing music out there at the stone door. I like these places I'm taking you to the best."

"Where are we going today?"

"I kind of wanted it to be a surprise again," he said smiling. "Is that okay?"

"Yeah, that's great," I smiled and looked out the window. I was blushing this time.

"Would you mind reaching into the glove box and handing me that jar of elderberry syrup?" he asked, clearing his throat.

"I didn't know you took elderberry."

"Every day," he said. "Well, I forgot to take it yesterday. I usually take it on my way to work every morning. That's why it's in the glove box."

I passed the bottle of syrup to him after loosening the lid. "My family makes a batch every year," I said. "I'll bring you some of ours to try."

"I like your family more and more."

I fell asleep and awoke somewhere close to Jamestown. Eventually, after some gravel roads and a short hike, we made it to some giant sandstone arches. I stopped underneath the first big arch and lay flat on my back, guitar resting on my stomach, and played softly. I hummed. A tear slid down into the earth. Tourists passed by and kids laughed. I scooted up and played all hunched over on my guitar for what seemed like an hour.

I finally stood and kept playing as I walked over and propped my back against the stone of the arch where it rested against the cool earth. The sound kicked around me, fluttering from the strings, my vocal cords ribbed and rising. Eventually, I stood and moved around, feeling through the music, until Kevin's back was pressed into mine, and my head rested against his spine. We played and sang as a small group of ten or twelve people formed around us. They swayed together as if they were one.

Peaches and Basil
Lyrics by Robin Ballard and Kevin Crenshaw

Peaches sang the blues
From sliding off the branch
And swelling in the heat.
Sweet sweat paired
to taste as cinnamon
Wrapped in creamy dough.
Basil bubbling in the heat.
Her heart beat
Makes his heat sweet.

It was troubling
to do dessert
With an unknown guest.
She's no stranger to confusion
in the delight
of sweet heat, sweet sweet heat...

Dandelions

Medicine for equilibrium, and to protect and coat the whole person in being one's self in each stage

The One
Cushion.
Puckerer's parachutes.
A wish. A kiss.
Next summer's walk.
Goldstone, smooth and cool,
Carry dew.
A furious rain bares down and washes
Pieces of gold in spring rivers.
Green and root to bestow.
Gold egg bread sizzles.
Crunchy perfume of the sun.
Hot taste of bloom.
Refreshing snap of green.
Warm salve of root.

Four | A Little Bit of Whiskey with My Hist'ry

CORA SHUFFLED AROUND Aunt Melinda's kitchen and the old Elvis room. She was making foods that weren't needed to feed a family of farmers, and when I brought a new cookbook with recipes from other cultures, she experimented and expanded her talent with food.

She said immediately that the dishes were "simpler." She placed a bowl of fresh salsa in front of me and said, "Reminds we of when I first learned to cook. I was just using what I had." She compared the whole food movement to the "go out and dig up something from the garden" movement of her youth. "That's the same thing as the 'go pick a piece of fruit off the tree' movement and the 'go grab a can of tomatoes from the cellar' movement in the wintertime." She laughed at her own wit and ran her hand through her white hair. She seemed more spry and alert than before, and I found myself wondering if she felt unburdened by telling the truth about being my great-grandma, Paul's mother. She seemed lighter and as if all of her communications were filled with humor and delight, as had her renewed joy for food.

I was still curious about all the family stories, so when Aunt Melinda asked me what I wanted for Christmas, as she always did early in the year, I told her that I wanted to have my DNA tested. I wanted to know what it would tell us about our lineage. I explained about the different companies I'd read about and how they just needed some spit to do it. Cora dropped the tea kettle into the sink with a loud clatter.

"Let me do that," Aunt Melinda said. "What kind are you making?"

"I guess we've still got some of the violet tea we blended, don't we?"

"Yeah, I reckon there's still plenty of it," Aunt Melinda answered and turned, giving me a quizzical look about Cora's odd reaction.

Cora exhaled loudly and then asked us, "Will it *really* tell you all that?"

"It's supposed to tell you a lot," I said. "It'll definitely show if there's any Native American or French in our background."

"So, we'll know if the stories are true or not?" she asked.

"Sort of," I said. "The DNA can't just say, 'You have an ancestor who was a Woods Runner.'

"Well, I know that," she interrupted me. "I was just thinking that I wouldn't mind having it done for myself."

"That's easy. I'll buy you both a spit analysis for Christmas," Aunt Melinda said and laughed. "Then, I'll know mine by looking at both of yours."

"My mama's DNA should still show up on mine," I said.

"Right," Aunt Melinda said. "Your daddy's part will match mine."

"You got any bread?" I asked Cora. My stomach was growling all of a sudden.

Aunt Melinda was waiting on pizza dough to set. Lately, they'd become hooked on it. They were always eating sourdough bread. Cora saved the starter for thirty years. Aunt Melinda told everyone and even did a segment on it for her morning show. Though most people associated the sourdough starter with loaves of bread, Aunt Cora used it to make pizza, muffins, crackers, rolls, and even cake. The starter had to be fed with more flour and water every so often, and when she did that, she removed part of the original starter. The part she removed was called cast-off. She didn't dare throw it out, and instead, she used it, most recently for pizza. I was so hungry that I thought I could eat a whole pizza by myself.

"You only come around here to eat all our food," Aunt Melinda teased me. "You know it's true, Aunt Cora. The little thing don't eat anything until she gets here. She saves up her hunger all day."

"That's right," Cora said, warming her hands over the stove eye while waiting for the tea. "Little teeny thing might float away but our food anchors her down."

"I need a bread anchor right now," I said.

"Got an English biscuit for you," Cora giggled.

"You wish it had turned out like that," Aunt Melinda teased her. "Way too much fluff to be called an English tea biscuit."

"New recipe?" I asked. "An English tea biscuit? One of those semi-sweet flat crackers?" I said dully and made a face.

Aunt Melinda buckled over laughing.

"Oh, stop it," Cora said. "You know you liked my scone-iscuits." She could hardly get the word out she was giggling so much. "Melinda ate every one of them already."

"You ate all of *what*?" I asked, not understanding what she was trying to say.

"Scone-iscuits!" Melinda roared. "That's what we've named them. They aren't scones. They aren't biscuits. They're—" and she waved her arms toward Cora who circled her wooden spoon in the air and said, "Scone-iscuits," again with a little singsong smile.

I laughed. "You two are too much," I said. "I need to move in."

"No!" they both shouted in unison and then cackled in laughter.

I pouted. They giggled. Well, actually, Aunt Melinda hugged her stomach and chortled.

"You know, I thought about something yesterday. An old recipe of Nenny's," Cora said, changing the subject. That perked me up and stopped Aunt Melinda from her continuous giggles that were getting annoying and making me pout even more.

"Dandelion fritters," Cora said with a little twinkle in her eyes. She swirled the spoon again and turned to whatever she had on the stove top, which emitted a smell of flowers frying in an iron skillet. When I peeked over, it looked like small beer-battered discs.

"Are you making that now?" I asked.

"Yes," she said. "I just had to have some."

"I want some," I said. "And I want the recipe for something. A surprise," I said before she could ask, "What for?"

"That'll be alright," she said.

"But back to my little self," I said, my stomach growling. "I can eat that whole skillet of those by myself. Do you have anything else right now?"

"You want this and that. Wanting everything. Fine," she said, even though she was happy about it. "I'll make you up something more than the fritters."

"Dandelion fritter?" I asked. "What's it taste like?"

"Crunchy sunshine," Cora smiled and placed some on a coffee filter so that the oil would drain away. She sprinkled them with a ground red spice. "See what you think," she said and passed the plate to me.

"What's that spice you put on there?" I asked. "Is it hot?"

"Sumac," she said. "No, not spicy. It's tangy."

The fritters were hot, so I blew on them for a moment and then bit into one. "A little floral sass," I said.

"I like that," Cora said and popped a couple in her mouth.

"What do you want me to do?" Aunt Melinda asked Cora. Melinda wanted to be helpful.

"Sit there and talk like you all do," Cora said, waved her spoon in the air toward us, and hummed as she started making a little feast. Aunt Melinda and I ate all the dandelion fritters before the tea was finished.

Cora hummed her song louder and stopped chopping leeks on the cutting board. I picked up the tune of "La Vie en Rose." She scooted her leeks into a big Dutch oven on the stove top. Steam was beginning to puff out of the kettle spout. She had already spooned the violet mixture into a tea ball that was in a teapot on the counter. The leeks sizzled and new steam rose up from the stove; she stirred them quickly and slid a lid over the top. She turned off the dial for the kettle before it whistled and poured the hot water into the teapot. She placed the lid over the top and steam escaped from the porcelain spout. Then, she placed the kettle on an iron trivet on the counter. She lifted the lid from the top of the teapot for a moment and held her face over it. She closed her eyes and inhaled as the steam covered her face in a light mist.

Aunt Melinda and I were silently watching Cora. She noticed the whole time but had continued on about her business as if she didn't notice us. Her motions were fluid and natural as a stream flowing through a ravine. The kitchen was her place of comfort. Maybe she thought that we'd eventually go back to talking, and we would, of course, but this time it took us longer than usual. She looked out of the corner of her eye for an instant and replaced the lid to the teapot, turned her back to us and slid back up on the stool.

Lifting the big metal lid of the Dutch oven with a potholder in her hand, she asked, "You forgetting something, ain't you?" Peering into the pot of leeks, her whole head was enveloped in a fog from the Dutch oven for a moment as if a towel were wrapped around it and then dissipated. I thought that she was talking to herself about what she was cooking. She cleared her throat, and I almost laughed out loud thinking that she was expecting those leeks and that Dutch oven to answer her.

"Me?" I heard Aunt Melinda asking, as if she was thinking the same thing that I was about Cora and it just dawned on her all of a sudden that Cora meant something else. "Me, yes, I am forgetting." Aunt Melinda was stammering, which wasn't like her at all. I looked confused back and forth between them. "I forgot, Robin, to ask you to come back tomorrow night for dinner, to meet Gordon's family."

"His family?" I asked. "You mean his daughter?" I already met Gordon a few times, when he came over for dinner, but *the families* hadn't met yet.

"Yeah, you know, he has a kid *and* a dog," Melinda said. "His daughter is all but grown and moved out, but yeah, he has two kids, counting the dog as one."

"Was he only married once?" I asked.

"Yep, just once before and divorced for a while now," she said and paused. "Robin." Her face turned red when she paused, and it wasn't from anger or embarrassment but from sadness, I thought. "I don't think there are many men who don't have kids and have never been married. If there are some, I haven't met them." She laughed awkwardly. "I always met the married ones until Gordon."

"Kept them around for too long," Cora said. "That's the problem." She pointed the wooden spoon at Aunt Melinda. "Gordon isn't married, so that's a step in the right direction."

"Stop it, Aunt Cora," Melinda said rolling her eyes toward me.

"You need to teach her so that she doesn't make the same mistakes," Cora said. She added seasonings and spooned a bowl of cooked potatoes into the leeks. "And start telling the truth. It will be good for you,

you'll see." Cora snickered, but Aunt Melinda kind of growled sitting there.

"Where'd you get those potatoes?" I asked Cora.

"Made them earlier," she said and poured something goopy from a little dish and a lot of milk into the pot.

"What are you putting in there?" I asked.

"Roux to make it thicker and some milk." She pinched up salt from a bowl three or four times and sprinkled it into the pot. Then, she placed a bowl on top of a plate. I grew impatient in my hunger knowing that she was planning to put the soup into the bowl and serve it to me soon.

Aunt Melinda wouldn't be distracted, and she was still groaning and growling a little. "It's alright," I said to her sensing that she might let Cora have it in her own way later. I continued, "I pretty much knew that something like that was going on with you, especially after the time we saw that woman in Castner Knotts with her daughter, and the daughter knew you, like knew you from the dad, and you tried to blow it off like she knew you from TV, but I could tell something was up."

"I forgot about that," Aunt Melinda said. "That was such a long time ago." She put her head in her hands.

Cora slid a teacup in front of each of us. She poured the tea, and I retrieved the cream from the refrigerator.

Aunt Melinda looked up. "Did I really wait that many years on him?" she asked Cora who had taken a seat at the table with her own teacup. "That many years?" Aunt Melinda repeated. "I was *that* woman, waiting around." She turned and looked at me, "Not for Gordon," she said. "It was someone else."

"This is good," Cora said. "Drink the tea. Tomorrow will be a great dinner for everyone. You'll see. Robin will be here with you. I'll be here."

"What about that soup?" I asked Cora while my stomach growled.

"Ten minutes," she said. "Drink the tea."

I wasn't looking forward to meeting Gordon's family. I was worried about his permanent presence limiting my time with my aunt in the future or changing her living arrangement with Cora. Yet, Cora didn't seem at all concerned about that and encouraged Melinda's relationship with Gordon. Maybe I was getting ahead of everyone.

Part of me didn't want to break up our little family that we had created since I moved to Nashville. I didn't want to picture the future when we would be doing something different. Sometimes I realized that Cora had been old for a very long time. And now, she seemed to be getting younger which scared the hell out of me. That type of change might mean something more, and I really didn't want to consider that just when we were all living this life together in ways that were liberating.

The following evening, I was so relieved to see that Gordon's daughter and dog weren't at the dinner. My Aunt Melinda took it personally, as if Gordon's daughter was judging her for being the other woman, even though her dad never had another woman. Gordon had never cheated on his wife, and he was proud of being honorable.

"Of course," he said. "My daughter already knows that I was faithful. She knows it." He was stressed. "She punishes both me and my ex for getting a divorce, still. That's why she took Knox today, so I couldn't even let you meet the dog," he said. He devoured a salad while venting about it. *He is an abandoned parent*, I thought.

I followed Gordon's lead with devouring the vegetables. I did enjoy the snap of a carrot and the crunch of lettuce as it twists. The bread was crispy with sound as well. Even Cora ate with more speed and gusto than usual. She even waved her hand, allowing us to get our own second helpings, giving up her station at the stove and kitchen counter in order to listen to Gordon's rant and watch him eat with such fervor. He was a thin man, but he ate with force. As he savored the food in these appreciative moments, that did captivate anyone sharing the table with him. He made me want to celebrate the enjoyment of my food more. Yet, he talked his way through it all.

"My daughter is still angry with both me and my ex. Honestly, she's used it as a tactic to manipulate both of us, and I'm not giving in anymore after this. I gave in tonight because I couldn't take it anymore, and I didn't want to put Melinda through the sulking and dagger eyes when she did nothing wrong. We can only feel guilty for so long."

We ate homemade pizzas. As the cheese drippings slid, Gordon's slurping tongue whistled in olives and onions. He closed his eyes, "Mmm.Mmm." Chewing with his eyes closed, he smiled, "Mmm." After swallowing, he opened his eyes wide and said, "I'm not sure why we feel guilty for being honest people who just don't want to be together anymore, me and my ex. And Melinda and I are honest people who want to be together." He growled and took a bite of the pizza. He chewed with anger until realizing how delicious the pizza tasted. He smiled and moaned again. Cora giggled.

"Manipulative!" he said opening his eyes again. Cora laughed. He looked at her and laughed, too. "I'm bitter about my divorce," he said. "But it's at Jamie, my daughter, and not my ex. She's actually cool, even to me and Melinda. It's fucked up."

I couldn't believe he said that to Cora, just straight on to a ninety-something year old lady whom he didn't know that well. I dropped my slice of pizza down the front of my shirt and made a mess. The hot cheese slid off. "Ah!" I shouted. Aunt Melinda jumped up and grabbed a dish towel, and then I knocked over our glasses of sweet tea. Cora sat there watching the whole thing unfold while laughing and then getting the giggles over it.

Gordon righted everything on the table while we cleaned up the mess on the floor, and Cora looked back and forth. Gordon said, "This is the best pizza. Really, the best I've had in the world. You could sell them. Maybe we should buy that old house restaurant and make it a pizza place?" He gestured as if the place were right outside.

"Gordon is trying to put you to work, Aunt Cora," Melinda said. "I've tried to tell him that Jamie's real problem with him is that he is constantly trying to put her to work. Sure, it's not like he's telling her to clean the house or work on a farm," she said leveling a gaze at Gordon over the edge of the table. It wasn't lost on us that they had already talked about this many times, and that it was a point of contention between them.

"Not at all the same," he said, wiping his mouth and throwing wet dish towels toward the laundry room off the kitchen.

"What old house restaurant?" Cora asked.

"He's asking her to build websites and who knows what he's coming up with to occupy her time," Aunt Melinda said, taking the wet towels from the floor to the laundry. "You know Jamie resents it, Gordon. Not everyone is as driven as you are."

"There's a place for sale up the road," Gordon said to Cora. "An old place, used to be a restaurant."

"I think it was a teahouse," Aunt Melinda corrected him. "But it hasn't been open in a really long time."

He refilled our tea glasses and then went right into defending his actions. "I would be so bored with shopping over and over again. She can shop every day, but why not choose something challenging? Build something? Create a business? I'm here offering to help her, and she shrugs and goes right back to some phone game where she trades computer purses. That's what she does with her time! Collect computer images?" He stared down at the pizza he was holding in his hand while he talked. "I can't talk about it anymore because it's spoiling the pizza."

Cora stood and put the kettle on the stove. "The old teahouse," she said. "It was a long time ago. I went one time. Mama took me and Jane."

We were silent. "Yes, I remember," Cora continued. "There was a psychic. Mama sat with her in the corner for a little spell while Jane and I drank a whole pot of tea and got the giggles from the sugar. Jane ate the cucumbers, and I tried to guess how they'd made all of those little treats." She caught her breath all of a sudden. "The scones," she said to Aunt Melinda. Tears puddled in her eyes suddenly. "I don't know why that's making me cry except maybe that was such a special day for me and Jane to be together there with Mama, and she wasn't pitting us against each other. She just enjoyed us each as we were."

"Do you know why she met the psychic?" I asked.

"Child, I don't have the faintest clue, and there's no telling," she said. "Knowing Mama, it could have been anything."

"How old were you?"

"I must have been round about fourteen," she said. "I was a teenager." She looked completely stumped. "I sure am shocked I didn't ever remember that even when Robin was doing them interviews. Now what do you think makes a person forget like that and then remember clear as can be?"

"I've often wondered the same thing," I said.

"Are you sure it was *that* teahouse?" Aunt Melinda asked, pointing in the direction of the teahouse.

"That's the funny thing," Aunt Cora said. "I've always thought it looked familiar, that old place, and I never could figure out why. It's been something I would puzzle over in my mind. Here's the answer as sure as Melinda said, 'teahouse.'"

"Well, I don't know," Aunt Melinda said. "But, Gordon wants to go in there and look at it."

Gordon shrugged, "I like good investments."

Cora shivered slightly. "I need a little whiskey after that memory." She stood and went to retrieve it from the cupboard.

"Well," Gordon laughed. "If you don't mind, Aunt Cora, I always need a little whiskey with my hist'ry."

"You might as well pour us a round," Aunt Melinda said to Cora.

That round was gone, and I was still trying to wipe the tomato stain off the front of my shirt but it was no use. I smeared it more.

"Let's get you a shirt," Aunt Melinda said and motioned for me to follow her.

"What's up?" I asked when we reached the spare room. I always kept clothes in the dresser there since I was a kid.

"Do you think Gordon will drive me crazy if I marry him?" she asked me like a sixteen-year-old wondering if she should accept a cute but obnoxious guy's invitation to prom.

"I don't know," I said shrugging. Rooting around in the dresser, I noticed that Gordon had moved into half of my dresser drawers. I grabbed a crumpled old Opryland t-shirt out and unfolded it. It smelled okay and contained one yellowed stain on the hem from something I couldn't remember.

"I'm taking this with me," I said, as I traded out my freshly stained shirt for the old Opryland one. This one had been Aunt Melinda's a long time ago and she gave it to me when I was little. It was faded in the center but you could still make out the picture of the pickers—a cartoon of a guitar player, fiddler, and banjo player underneath the words, "Home of the Pickers." On the bottom of the shirt were the words

Opryland USA. The red trim on the neck and the sleeves looked good on me.

"I'm surprised it's still here," she said. "You ought to wear that on stage. I almost can't believe it."

"I bet you got all kinds of good vintage clothes like this in those boxes stacked in the back of your closet and don't remember," I said.

"Don't get any ideas," she said. "But yeah, there are some things in there that would be great for the stage." She turned in a circle. "I can't think straight because I've been worried about what to do with Gordon," she said.

"Why do you have to do anything?" I asked. "Did he already ask you to marry him?"

"No, he hasn't, but he's been hinting about it," she said. "I can feel that it's coming." She walked to the little walk-in closet and clicked on the light overhead. She disappeared into the back of it.

"Wait until he actually asks you," I said. "And just see what pops out of your mouth."

"That's one way to deal with it," she said shouting back over her shoulder while scooting hangers quickly. "But no, no, no, that is not me. I'm independent and have always been. I don't even like worrying about a man this much, and that makes me afraid of how much I'm going to have to be worrying about this man and his family if I marry him."

She emerged carrying a short white lace dress. "Here," she said, holding the dress out to me. It was clearly vintage and in the style of Twiggy. The sleeves were long and sheer lace with fringed cuffs. "You think you might ever have a venue where you'd wear this one? One that's mod enough? I've been meaning to give it to you for a while now, but I hadn't dragged it out of the back of the closet yet. I knew it had to be back there. I wore it one time on the show when we had a '60s tribute about twenty years ago. They gave me the dress. They used to give me a lot of clothes, but now everything I wear is sponsored so they take it back right after we film the shows."

I held the dress up in front of me and inspected the sleeves and the lace. There wasn't one tear or snag in the lace. Even the designer's tag from the '60s on the inside of the neck was in excellent condition. I tried the zipper and it worked well, though I had to take my time so that none of the lace got caught in the teeth.

"You like it?" she asked while nodding her head up and down.

"You know I love it," I said. "It's going to be so cute with the right boots."

"And jewelry," she said. "Brown and turquoise would be great colors with it." I nodded in agreement. She covered the dress with the plastic again and handed it back to me.

We stood there in silence. "Thank you," I said.

She said, "Of course," immediately and we started to go back to the kitchen.

I stopped. "Maybe you can work out an alternative arrangement with Gordon," I said. "I hear about people now who are married but they don't live together. They have other arrangements."

She nodded. "That's not a bad idea. Something unique." I could see her mind spinning those ideas into different scenarios.

"Or don't get married," I said. "You can still stay together." I placed the dress and my dirty shirt by the front door, and we joined them in the kitchen again.

Voices chattered from the radio mounted to the wall. It was tuned to public radio. As we took our seats, I could hear the news reports. Cora had set the table for tea and dessert. Gordon's face hovered just over the top of his teacup and his eyes were closed. When he opened them, he stared at my t-shirt. "I haven't seen one of those in a long time," he said. "You're going to wear it for a show?"

"Yeah, we were saying that it would be great on stage," I said.

He leaned in and stared at the shirt. "Unbelievable," he said. "You had this?" he asked Melinda.

"Yeah, but it's Robin's shirt," Aunt Melinda said. "I forgot about it. I gave it to her when she was little. She'd wear it every time she came to visit."

While we talked, Cora spooned out strawberries over shortcakes she'd baked earlier. They were on individual saucers. She took a bowl of fresh whipped cream from the refrigerator and spooned some over everyone's dessert. Gordon dipped his finger into the whipped cream and tasted it. "You made this whipped cream?" he asked.

"Certainly," she answered. "I made all of it." She smiled and took a bite, not waiting for anyone else to dig in. We were all waiting for her to start. After her first bite, she took a sip of tea.

Gordon turned to me, "Do you have a guitar here?"

"Nah, but I've got a mandolin," I said.

"Would you mind playing something for me?" he asked. "Maybe you know it."

"If I know it," I said and went to the bedroom to get the mandolin. I clicked off the radio when I returned.

"It's Bill Monroe," he said.

"Okay, which one?" I asked and settled onto the edge of my chair.

"Mule Skinner Blues?"

"Gooooood mooornin,' Captain." I sang and played. Gordon laughed and they listened. Cora sang, and she even went for a yodel. Gordon clapped his spoon in time.

"Yeah!" Cora shouted when I finished.

"Brilliant," Gordon said.

"Thank you, Robin," my aunt said.

I nodded and picked around a little before putting the mandolin down in an empty chair.

"You know 'Mule Skinner' is one of those songs that's been recorded by so many people," I said. "It's a Jimmie Rodgers song, originally."

"Didn't realize that," Gordon said. He snapped his fingers, trying to think of something.

"Woody Guthrie made a record of it, too," Cora said, looking off in the distance, as if listening to him. "Little water boy, bring your water round." She sang lightly and smiled.

"That mint smells wonderful," Aunt Melinda inhaled the steam from her cup and continued. "It takes me back to the farm every time, to that patch of mint that Hoot and Ma Zona kept out back. I loved that chocolate mint."

"That's what this is, child," she said. "Yeah, Robin brought me the chocolate mint plants last year sometime and I got a container full out there on the sun porch. I had to give it a bigger pot this winter, it grew so fast."

"I never realized you had chocolate mint growing out there," Aunt Melinda said.

Everyone took a sip of tea and inhaled the fragrance deeply. "I planted that mint they kept at the farm," Cora said. "I was the one brought in all the kinds of mint and sage and no telling what else."

"Where'd you get the plants?" Melinda asked.

"About near everywhere," Cora said. "I traded seeds with some people. I got some from my aunt, Delores, when she visited. She was traveling and going places that I didn't ever get to go to, but she'd bring me back all sorts of roots and seeds. Sometimes, I got something to grow for just a little bit and it died, but plenty of times, I got those plants to grow and I was the only one that would have some of the cultivars around us. My mama and daddy, they loved thinking we had something that nobody else had, and Daddy would ask me to infuse that shine and whiskey with them herbs. Sometimes, it was really good, and powerful hard to duplicate it every time. The plant is different with every growing season. It might be the same plant, corn, even the same variety of corn, but like my daddy said, 'that corn isn't the same from last year and won't be the same next year.' That's always the truth of making something with plants. The shine, the food, the tea; no batch is going to taste exact the same." She took a big bite of her strawberry shortcake and looked to be sure that we were each eating ours.

She smiled with satisfaction after seeing that everyone's bowl was empty except hers.

"Fascinating," Gordon said, smiling at Aunt Melinda.

"What other herbs are in this tea?" I asked.

"Oh, some wild things like that ground ivy, blackberry leaves, and I can't recall what else in this one."

"You could sell this, too," Gordon said.

"The shortcakes or the tea?" I asked him.

"Both," he said. "Absolutely everything you make, you could sell."

Aunt Melinda got up and went to the counter for more shortcake, but Gordon thought her movements signaled a criticism of his statements. "I guess this is just my way of complimenting someone," he said defensively. "Encouraging business." Aunt Melinda didn't act as though she noticed. Her mind seemed to be somewhere else.

"Thank you for the compliments," Cora said. "If I wasn't almost a hundred, maybe I would open a restaurant." Her mouth stretched into a huge grin. Gordon settled back in his chair and returned her smile. Both felt validated by the other.

"You all making it okay in the van?" Gordon asked me, changing the subject. "Are you getting the equipment and everything in it?"

"Yeah." I blew into the tea even though it wasn't that hot. "We have a lot booked for the summer, so I'm taking most of my stuff back to Miss Emy's. I moved into the spare bedroom at Angie's place."

"That's a good plan," Gordon said. "Your aunt is still trying to get you a record deal." Aunt Melinda slapped his arm.

"You aren't supposed to tell her that," she said and blushed.

"Please, don't, Aunt Melinda," I said. "I feel bad that it's not working out."

"That's the way it is," Gordon said. "She's doing the right thing for you." He nodded to my aunt and then smiled. "Gotta keep asking and talking. That's how most people get their deals." Gordon was an investor. He helped people start businesses that would otherwise probably not exist.

"Well, thank you," I said and sank into my chair.

I looked at Cora, and she nodded. I worried about her even though she moved with greater ease in the past two years. Truthfully, due to her age and not her conditions, I thought about her death often. She knew the details of all the spaces of Aunt Melinda's house, so she was comforted by knowing where her feet would land, how hot the stove burned, how far to turn the dial on the water to get a perfect temperature, and how many laps to walk around the yard to keep her body moving into the next day. I reminded myself of her strength.

"I'm sleepy now," she said. "You'll make a record soon. They'll both help you." She smiled and stood.

"Thank you, Aunt Cora," I said. "I love you."

"I love you." She patted my head.

"Thank you for the most delicious meal," Gordon said, stood and bowed toward Cora. She giggled and waved her hand at him.

"Good night," Aunt Melinda said, reaching out her hand and patting Cora on the backside as she passed.

Cora carried her tea toward her room. At the doorway, she called, "Good night and sweet dreams, everyone."

Ten o'clock the next morning, an urgent banging hammered on the apartment door. Since it was Sunday, I had slept in. The loud banging wouldn't stop. Angie shouted that it was for me. I moved slowly, but once I saw Aunt Melinda's face, I knew it. She was there to tell me. The strangest sensation washed over me. She reached her hands out to mine and looked into my eyes.

"Aunt Cora passed in her sleep last night," she said through choked tears. She sobbed. "I never wanted to find her, but of course, I always knew that I would. She didn't come in the kitchen and Gordon left. I wanted him to leave so bad because I just knew something was wrong. I kept thinking that she didn't like him being there, but it wasn't that."

I let Aunt Melinda talk and talk. "I called. They sent an ambulance anyway because they have to confirm that she's dead. They promised me that she passed peaceful. The woman paramedic said that her little ticker just run out..." She stopped and breathed deeply, wiping tears and then blowing out a breath. "I love her," she said, chin quivering. "Little ticker," she laughed. "She would have got a kick out of that, but I'm sad." Aunt Melinda dropped her face into her hands.

"I know," I said. "I know how much you're going to miss her."

"I've got to call Miss Emy," she said suddenly dismissing her own grief. "And, everybody." She threw up her hands. "I wanted to tell you first."

That did it. I cried and hugged her, vowing to help her call everybody, which wasn't that many people after all. I did put off calling one person in particular, though I couldn't say exactly why. Miss Emy stopped me from having to deal with it and said, "I'll call your daddy, but don't expect him to be there."

I was afraid to ask why. The silence stayed until the phone static was loud. I swallowed, and my face burned hot.

"Is he back in rehab?" I asked.

"Yeah," she said. "He'll be alright though."

A Little Bit of Whiskey with my Hist'ry
Lyrics by Gordon Bell and Robin Ballard

...That sad old story was part of everyone's glory
Those days when they were makin' hay and thought of
hero's stories as their own. But as the years passed, she
grew bitter and hated all the pain that place was known
to bring, so she cheated, she hated, she hurt and she
berated everyone, herself and everyone. ...
She was destined for a tragedy. And it came to pass.
Yeah, what she saw came to be...

Ever since then, I've always needed a little whiskey with
my hist'ry, just to get down to the bottom of the story,
there's no glory. Only pain and heartache.
That pain and heartache just won't go...

Wood Sorrel

Medicine for a positive presence in all places

Zinger of the wood line,
Of the grass by the porch,
Under the pasture fence.
Bright fruit of clover cousin,
Lucky for taste and accompaniment,
Merry-making with time in your stride.
The ease of all seasons, all friends, serving
Every course—a brightness to salad,
A sauce to fish, a spread to crust,
A delight with fruit. Treasure trove.

Five | Cowbird Blues

GHOSTS LIVE EVERYWHERE. On each square inch of this planet, something has lived and died. The ghosts' imprints are all over everything, but you've got to get the right light to fall on those footprints in the dewy grass of morning before you can see them.

My daddy was in love with Westerns. He watched them all the time, whether he was high or not. Some stuff didn't interest him when he was high like it did when he was sober and vice versa, but Westerns made the cut no matter what his state of mind. Usually, he would chill out and watch the show, even if he was obnoxious and wanted interaction, depending on his mood. There were times when I had no idea whether he was stoned, and I mean rocked out internally because he got so used to it. Really, there were times when it wasn't like you'd think. He was shooting up plenty, and I have these real memories I can't believe that I'd completely forgotten about, and they'll resurface.

We'd be watching a Western and someone would start playing a guitar, and he'd get so excited if I could pick out part of what they were playing on my guitar. He'd ask me to do it with songs on the radio, too. I tried hard to get it right because it kept him occupied and made him happy. My proud moments were showing him that I had figured out the opening theme song to his favorite show. He grinned and said, "You got you an ear, don'tcha, girl?"

These memories startle me with how I forgot so much. They are a scary kind of *how could I possibly forget seeing that and tell myself that I remembered and had what people call a good memory*? Bragging about my stable and reliable brains? Maybe I was only trying to deeply reassure myself. Either way, I really thought it—that I had some kind of elephant's memory until unbelievable resurfacing was there in the snap of a finger. Examples kept coming, making me wonder about these brains we possess with their potential to conjure a remembrance that should have been filed under comfortable shock, but becomes filed into the darkest corner, and not even because something happened in a weird way.

No, it's just a time of being with my daddy, watching Ben Cartwright and Matt Dillon have shootouts on TV, and knowing that I saw my dad shoot up when I walked in on him accidentally, and turning abruptly and going back to watch the show. Knowing how chill my dad was, happy even. He was cool because he had the money to get a fix that allowed him to be relaxed and entertained and nice to be around for a while. He wasn't out of control or obnoxious all the time. I never understood what all the fuss was about if he already had what he needed, but I came to understand that when he had heroin, he was *his kind of normal*.

I questioned it even as I grew older and I knew for certain that he was sober and working to help other people get that way, too. The questions had been my way of life, my way of surviving him and knowing when to retreat and when to scurry forward. Sometimes, I enjoyed being around him and we did laugh and discuss the finer points of whether the posse was going to ride out over the frontier, and who was secretly a cheat and how to read their mannerisms. Other times, I just quietly watched, sun warming through the window and me falling asleep, low voices becoming stern and fading away.

My child self couldn't see his addiction clearly because he didn't have a terminal illness like cancer. Nothing looked to be wrong with him, and no doctors had even told my child self that he needed some kind of a medication for anything I knew to be a real sickness or disease. Yet, he seemed pretty sick a lot.

It took years before I processed what addiction really was, what it meant. I was confused, and withdrawing was more essential than most other actions.

My daddy loaded up his truck one morning and then strolled inside the farmhouse, told me to "pack up a bag, and get in the truck." I was sure that he had decided to take me back to live with my mama's people, that they still lived somewhere over in the corner of the county. I recalled Miss Emy's description that they were a "not so nice group that pretended briefly to pine away for your little mama, but they're too rowdy a bunch to come see you. Can come anytime they want to right over here to us on the Ridge 'cause nobody's leaving you over there." She was as territorial as a raptor with that fan going while she talked.

I remember packing a bag but not what I put in it. I just recall that Daddy yelled back in the door, "Put on your cowgirl boots and hat!" I can vividly see those boots swinging in the truck. And those boots on the pavement by the side of the interstate after we stopped to pick up a hitchhiker whose broken down Camaro belched out black smoke. With the toe of my boot, I scratched at the gravel that was on the side and wandered down into the grass towards a wide field with a white clapboard tall house, kind of like Miss Emy's in the distance and a barn, and a wooden fence smiling broad in the sunlight. I picked some wood sorrel I found and ate a few strands. I always liked the lemony flavor and how quickly they dissolved, like candy almost. I shoved a handful of sorrel into my pocket.

"Come on!" Daddy yelled and waved for me to get back in the truck. "Scoot over in the middle," he said. "We're giving this guy here a ride into Knoxville."

"Thank you for stopping to give me a lift," the guy said. He was about twenty, a couple years older, maybe. His t-shirt draped away from his body. He was sweating. He removed the sunglasses from his face and slicked back his long brown hair. "You happen to have a napkin or a handkerchief in here?" he asked my daddy. He dripped, his smile melted down at me, and my daddy motioned to the glove box and shifted gears.

"You're welcome," Daddy said. "It's too bad about your car."

He took a washcloth from the glove box and wiped his face with it and replaced his sunglasses. "Man," he said, exasperated, sweat slipping down his sunglasses. "That Camaro was supposed to make me cool. Here I am stranded on the side of the road pouring sweat. Is it the Fourth of July or something? Man, it's hot."

I laughed, thinking that he was joking. "Course it's the Fourth of July," I said. "Me and Daddy are going on a vacation." I picked a clover-shaped strand from my pocket and ate it.

"Seriously?" he asked. "The actual Fourth of July?" I knew right away that he wasn't a good actor, so he wasn't faking it. He did not know the date. My daddy nodded and lit a cigarette. The hitchhiker glanced down at me, and in our exchange, I knew that I read the man's signals correctly.

"Yeah, buddy," Daddy said exhaling his smoke. "Fourth."

"Man," the hitchhiker said and ran his hands through his hair and blew out a bemused breath, stumped. Beads dispersed in the air, in the light, drizzled the dash in front of him, the radio player. "I been down there in Summertown and damn near lost track of time," he said, then slapped his leg, moisture printed with his hand on his thigh. A slight squish, and I winced into my daddy at the sound. The man laughed with one of those, I-cannot-believe-in-all-my-years-of-being-alive-that-this-human-brain-just-truly-lost-track-of-time.

"I did lose track of time!" he said, giving my daddy a wild look, and he bellowed with laughter again. I scooted even closer to my daddy who laughed a little with him and wasn't so sure about him, villain or the good guy with an odd way of laughing or crying, living or lying, *crazy?* We were on our own time trail, boots ready, eyes trained. My daddy seemed to speed up just a little bit.

"You eating clover?" the man asked me, as if he suddenly noticed that I picked the stems from my pocket and as if I might be the one who was a little crazy.

"No, it's sorrel," I said.

"What are you making up?" he asked. "I saw you pick it from the side of the road back there, in the clover."

"It's sorrel," Daddy said. "Looks similar, but it's not the same as clover. Sorrel is edible. You want a cigarette?" Daddy asked him. "You like bluegrass?" Daddy asked a follow-up question, pressed play on the cassette, and turned up the volume on "On and on."

I was glad when the man said "yes," to the cigarette because I wanted him to reflect and look out the window and drift off with the smoke from his cigarette, even if it did stink double since they were both smoking.

"What's it taste like?" he asked me. "Sorrel?"

"Lemons," I said and handed him a wilting and sweaty strand. He ate it and smiled.

"Open up the glove box again," Daddy instructed him. "And find one of those fans in there. You see one?" He rifled through the papers, snacks, and slid one of Miss Emy's church fans out.

"This?" he asked looking a little disgusted and amused at the same time. He seemed like he might be afraid of Jesus, which made me giggle though I tried to suppress it.

"That's the one," Daddy said. "You see on the back of it, there's a calendar. You take it with you from now on and you'll know when it's the Fourth of July, plus you'll have a fan when it's hotter'n hell outside." My daddy laughed and the man laughed with him. They both smoked their cigarettes in mostly quiet until we arrived at a gas station. I remember that my daddy gave him a whole pack of smokes and wouldn't let him forget the fan when he almost left it behind in the floorboard.

"You'll thank me someday," Daddy said, tipped his hat, and we drove away and turned the radio up to overcome the sound of our roaring muffler.

I wondered a few times in my life about that hitchhiker. If he threw the fan away and then wished he had it back. If he kept it and watched it save his ass again and again from minor hells. I imagined him being freaked out about it arriving at times—a talisman, a gift of Southern travelers strangely perplexing, printed with hippie Jesus in the desert, footprints, lily flowers below him or beside him, walking, valley of the shadow. Or, if somewhere in between when he got his Camaro from the side of the road and when he became a corporate dad in the nineties, it vanished and no one thought of it except me ever again.

Daddy picked up hitchhikers a few times on that trip. Out of Knoxville, we let in a woman who was holding a cardboard sign that said, *Coastal Bound*.

"We aren't goin' that far," Daddy said. She said it was alright and would take whatever stretch of road we offered. She hopped up beside me, handing me a piece of bubblegum from her pocket.

We gave two teenagers a ride out of Ghost Town on our way back. They told Daddy that they'd been on the road for years, and he said, "Cowbirds." They looked puzzled as if he might be insulting them. "Yep, cowbirds are born hitchhikers," he continued. "The cowbird parents sneak and lay their eggs in the nests of other birds, and then those other birds raise 'em, you know give 'em a ride, so to speak, until they grow up to fly out on their own."

"I like that," one of the boys said. He elbowed his friend or his brother, I don't recall if they were related. "We're a pair of cowbirds," he said, smirking. "That's right clever of them birds."

I wondered what it meant in my own life sometimes. Then, I thought about the whole trip as I was planning a new one. At Ghost Town in the Sky, I had looked down from the chair lift and watched my cowgirl boots dangle over the mountains beside my daddy's.

Yes! I had been on a rollercoaster with my daddy, but what happened? Why did this memory return out of nowhere? I worried about events that I couldn't remember because I tried to block out parts of my childhood. I went to have a candid conversation with my friend who I didn't think would judge and who was quickly becoming a real best friend and band mate. I asked Angie what she thought. I'd always attributed my first and only amusement park experience to Opryland with Aunt Melinda. Then, this memory with my dad happened. I recalled it as if it was yesterday.

"Well, most of it," I said to Angie. "I don't know why I didn't remember it before. It has nothing to do with Cora dying, but it's like her death triggered the memory. And, I was like *him*, Mr. Fourth of July, the hitchhiker. I'm beside myself in disbelief that I didn't remember. Why did I suppress it or forget or whatever I did? What did I do?"

"You might have done all of those things," Angie said. "I don't know. Keep telling the story and see where it leads you." She sucked in a breath and then said, "Sorry to say, but it's probably more about your dad being in rehab again. *Maybe* you'll discover some other answer for why you chose to forget it until this stage in your life. But you know, Robin, you might not have chosen for any reason at all. Maybe you just forgot. You *were* only five?"

"Yes, but I even saw a bear," I said to her. "I remember seeing a real bear in a cage. People were paying. I can't remember why. It was a big bear...by the side of the road in a cage, as if it's another time period or something? But it was real. It actually happened and I, I, forgot about it. It comes roaring back up, so bright and vivid, and for what?"

"Have you ever seen a bear since that time?" Angie asked.

"No," I said. "Never again. You know I did call Miss Emy just to make sure I wasn't crazy. I asked her if my daddy ever took me on a vacation to Ghost Town in the Sky, and she said, 'Oh, yes, probably more than once. He loved that place. He was a little obsessed for a couple of years and I thought he was plumb crazy for running the roads for all that Western stuff. I guess that it would have been better for him to have stayed addicted to that place than what came after it. You know, I bet that was his escape after your Mama died and before he got so caught up into heroin. I 'spect he already tried the drugs, but it wasn't nothing like it would become.'"

"Robin," Angie said. "Maybe you've forgotten because everything that happened after that was so harsh. It's exactly like your grandmother says for him. He needed an escape. She would have made a great psychiatrist, by the way. To the point. I should know, I've had to go to therapists my whole life."

"Really, your whole life for...You think so?" I asked. "Miss Emy has it figured out?"

Angie shrugged and chuckled. "My mom had a life coach and spiritual therapist for me for a while. You have no idea how much *counsel* I've had."

"No wonder you're easy to talk to."

"Yep, practiced," she smiled.

"Well, that's good, I guess, and gives me some relief for sure," I said.

"Why do you say it gives you relief?"

"Because basically, like you, Cora was always telling me that I have all the answers inside of me if I'll only just listen to them. Pay enough attention to read people. Plus, she said that my daddy was not as bad as I think he was."

"Only you know that," Angie said and shrugged.

The No How Blues
Lyrics by Robin Ballard

It's a no good, no account story,
It ain't got no glory,
No how,
No, no, no, no, no how.

It's a real bad story 'bout a cowboy
But he ain't got no glory,
No how
No, no, no, no how.

He was goin' to steal
When it turned a bad deal,
For nothin'
All for nothin'
He was good for nothin'
All for nothin'

He can't remember a thing
Don't know how he got that ring
On his finger here
His recollection ain't clear.
He said, "I don't even know where I come from, dear."
Memory's good for nothin'
All good for nothin'
Cain't remember nothin'
Ain't that somethin'
Now, ain't that somethin'

He's not a cowboy for real
He's a cowbird, that's the deal,
Dropping in, no invite,
Hitching a ride through the night.
For nothin'
All for nothin'.

He shot and he killed
The mule that tilled
For nothin'

All for nothin'
He's good for nothin'
All for nothin'

In his saddle, I took my share
He don't deserve this mare
No how
No, no, no, no, no how.

I aimed my gun
Said "Gimme your boots"
And made him run
For nothin'
No, no, no, no, no how. Not for nothin' no how...

Chamomile

Medicine for gentle rest, to imagine, to daydream

This lawn flower
Enchantress of the garden
Becomes a tea, a power
Releaser of alluring remedies
To rest in ease
Restless fragrance
Soft pillows to appease
Greens rising from the dirt and laid open.
Eases a gaseous stomach, a troubled head,
As cold lacy cushions in July. The fairy lights
Nightmares that cause dread,
Whorled in towers, drooping white
And offer a drowsy antidote
Lying underneath, quilting the clouds
To gentle rest afloat
Pollen points. Blessed day and dreams
A dreamland seascape.
Steeped from the love of roots, rabbits, heat thrashing
The smoke on the landscape
Into your cup of flowers, moons
Calmly wafting
Stars. Cradling you as you rest
The soft flowers' offering.
In the chamomile lawn.

Six | Family Medicine Wheel Breakdown

WHEN I WANTED to think for a while, I drove the long way to Granville and it always seemed like my problems unraveled in my mind as I went. I took the back roads, which was every bit of an hour longer since they added traffic lights on some of them, and a couple of crossings through towns showed that those places weren't so little anymore. It used to be maybe a fifteen minute difference. I didn't care though, as I wanted to soak everything in and listen with the windows rolled down on my way. I was full of life, and the countryside was loud and bright on the high points and thick and resonant in the lows. I stuck my hand out of the rolled down window and allowed the air currents to raise and lower my arm, roller-coastering it in the wind. Sometimes, it felt like a little bug flicked against it or a particle drifting on the breeze scraped by.

That day was blustery, and my car bounded up and whipped back down the hills, arriving at Miss Emy's faster than I had expected. The day was searing, all the blooms ruffling out to cover the earth, and the places around the house, where even shadows usually hid, were exposed. The farm didn't seem to like being straightened and slicked back. It rippled in trees and gardens, grasses and thorns. Every time I arrived, I was struck by how alive it was. An immediate swarming. After being in the city for so many years while in college, I'd gotten used to the tame nature that was around me there. Even Cora forgot sometimes and made a big deal over her small patch of mint, that strip of sunflowers Melinda always planted out front, the herbs on the back porch, the sun porch filled with flowers, a honeysuckle cluster on the chain link fence, and her four pear trees in the back yard. She took an inventory of her plants and "wild ones" as she called them.

It suddenly occurred to me that Cora hadn't been back to this place, what I call Miss Emy's place, in who knows how long, and this was where she grew up and she fell in love with Harold Flynn. To Cora, the farm wasn't Miss Emy's place at all, but it was her parents' house, the old home place. *This place*, I thought, everything saturating me, coming back up and onto me, all that I knew now and hadn't told anyone about Cora, her big confession to me—that she was actually my great-grandmother and *not* my great-aunt—and I waited. I didn't know why I was standing there waiting. Some passage was happening under the surface. I felt the awareness of all that I'd been through, all I'd been preoccupied with since going to college, and how I didn't even think I would go to college when I lived in this house, how clueless and lost I was.

I could feel her, my previous self, that girl who half grew up in these walls, standing before me. I saw us running to the other house, the smoke, all that smoke and heat and popping, crashing, roaring of a fire. I thought of Miss Emy, and for the first time realized she experienced two significant house fires: The first that killed her mama, and the second that was set purposefully by her son. The ways we related to one another, both of us without a mother. I had forgotten how loud the fire was when the other house was burning, the one that I had thought of as mine and my daddy's house.

I realized that this was just me growing up, becoming aware of the changes in life, the passage of time showing its face to me as if a clock rang inside of me somewhere and reminded me to give pause, to stop and notice the shifts, the subtle growth, the shocks that I couldn't have expected. It was all that tangle of plants that spoke, offering the medicine, I thought, as I looked at the growth, all bunched up and packed around the porch. The plants were the clock, with their rattle of rose hips in the fall, their crunch of leaves, their hum from bees combing through flowers, their swaying and rustling in the winds. They were the real signal. I parted the hydrangeas and followed the walk that was crumbled and grassy, violet sprinkled, and damp with shade that never dried out completely.

I could feel Cora, too. Yet, the plants and trees wouldn't have been the same. Maybe a couple, here and there, something she would recall and just so she could say it was the same. I knew right then that maybe I should have made the effort to bring Cora back to the farm last year. It could have been a surprise. I pictured it. But, then immediately, I wondered, *why*? Why hadn't she asked to return? Was it that painful? I almost heard it on the wind, and in my spine, it straightened 'cause I did hear it there, *Ghosts*. She'd be seeing the ghosts, their filmy shadows running around, their sounds becoming a little too audible, and their dewy footprints leading to memories.

"I thought you's leaving tomorrow." I jumped back when I heard the voice so close by. Miss Emy spoke from a stilled rocking chair on the porch, staring at me. I realized that she'd been watching me the whole time, fan shushed in her lap so she could spy on me quietly as long as she wanted. I guess she decided I wasn't going to do anything interesting, and she interrupted my staring.

"Damn it! Miss Emy! You could've said something!" I yelled at her, even though we hadn't seen one another since the funeral.

"I did," she said, looking aggravated. She smiled after that and began rocking and waving her fan. "Well, are you leaving tomorrow or not?" she asked.

"No," I said, still irritated. "It's a few days away, and I came out here to see you before I go."

"That was awful sweet of you," she said. "I'm glad you come. What time do you leave?"

"Thursday afternoon," I said. "We're driving to Atlanta and have a few stops on the way. Chattanooga, first."

"Oh," she stopped and clucked her tongue. "Chattanooga first. I think you've got a good band. I like the CD you gave me at Cora's funeral. I think it's as good as anything you hear on the radio now. It should be on the radio all the time, in my opinion. Needs more songs. Two is not enough."

"I'm glad you think so, Miss Emy. That's just a demo, not a full album."

"I'm not just saying that 'cause you're my granddaughter. Now, I really mean it. People say all these same things all the time, but I'm not somebody to jibber jabber flattery."

"I know, and I thank you."

"Are you coming in or needing to do something out in the yard?" After she said it, she folded her fan and paused while staring me down. I didn't know what she was thinking about, as I had forgotten about the metal detector times.

"Why are you looking at me like that?" I asked.

She smirked and started her fan again, "You here to dig in the ground?"

I rolled my eyes. "Whatever," I said. "You wouldn't be teasing if we'd gone and dug up where the metal detector went off. There's probably the treasure right there in the medicine wheel and, thanks to Aunt Melinda, we've abandoned it."

She ignored me, pursed her lips, and motioned with the fan. "Well, come on and sit on the porch or go inside and fix you something to eat," she said. "I've got some leftover biscuits and chocolate gravy in there. I must have felt that you was coming because I don't never make it for myself anymore. I had a craving all day long, so I whipped some up. I couldn't eat but one of them, and the rest is still sitting in there. Don't that beat all?" She smiled and waved me onto the porch with her fan and pointed with it toward the screen door.

I walked onto that big wide porch, the stretch of it, the solidity of it. How many generations lived in the rooms beyond, and all the people they had brought into its walls, who walked up onto the porch, knocked upon the door or just came right on inside, and how it had passed down through the generations to welcome new life, new sorrows, tragedy, music. I saw myself playing on the porch, practicing on the steps, mosquitoes pressing me inside, wrapped in blankets during the winter, the time I threw the guitar down the stairs, how I tripped and busted my lip once, and where I passed in and out of the halls without ever taking note of its structure and grace. Even when I wrote about this house for the class in college, I was collecting data about it.

Leaving for the trip pressed the feelings of appreciation upon me, as if I were homesick in advance, as if I already knew what it was going to mean to feel the beauty of what I had in life. I couldn't say what was going to give it to me or why or how, except that I knew it was coming from the experience of the trip.

As usual, as if she were reading my mind, Miss Emy said, "All this will be right here when you get back. I'll be holding down just fine like I been doing most of my life." She stilled the rocking chair and her fan. "You'll need to heat up those biscuits a little, but not too much if you use the microwave. The oven is better if you're willing to wait a spell for them." She stood and followed me inside.

I turned on the gas under the stove eye to heat the chocolate gravy in the iron skillet and covered it again with the lid so that it would heat up faster. Miss Emy supervised nearby, but not too close, to be sure I still did everything the way that she taught me. I lit the oven. I placed two biscuits in another iron skillet, slid some butter between them without crumbling them to pieces, and put them in the oven. I added another pat of butter to the chocolate gravy heating on the stove. I turned it on low and waited. Miss Emy smiled, pleased.

Her fan went back and forth with ease. It pushed a sweet fragrance toward me, and I looked around to find its source. Behind her on the counter, I saw a small mason jar holding the little wild roses.

"Those roses smell perfect."

"They bloomed a little early this year, I think, but I could smell them on the wind. I tracked 'em down and cut a spray."

We stood in silence for a moment, only Miss Emy's fan making a whaa, whaa, whaa, whaa. Finally, she stopped its movement for a moment. "You looking forward to playing in Atlanta?" she asked.

"Yeah," I said. "But, I felt like a little bit of a dummy when I had to tell everyone that I've never been anywhere. Like nowhere but Nashville and Gatlinburg. Oh, and after I talked to you, I realized that I've been to North Carolina, technically, cause Ghost Town in the Sky was in North Carolina."

"I don't think it was," Miss Emy said. "That's Cherokee that you're thinking about, and you probably did go there with your daddy, too, so you've been to North Carolina either way. I do think that Ghost Town was in Tennessee though, and you're just getting them mixed up."

"Nope, I looked it up, Miss Emy. It was definitely in North Carolina. That's the one other place I've been before the band, so I had to make sure. You can't try and take my extra state away from me or make it stand on a technicality," I said, joking.

"Well, I reckon that I never realized either of those things," Miss Emy said. "Ghost Town being in North Carolina, and that you had never been out of Tennessee really." Her fan rested on her folded arms, and it made me realize that her fan sometimes rested when she was thinking and sometimes it went crazy while she was worrying over something. *Maybe Miss Emy's memories were a resting fan*, I thought.

"Me and your Aunt Carolyn took the kids to the beach that summer," she said. "I could have swore that you went with us." Her fan started up again. She was using an accordion style fan that day. It was made of teakwood and contained designs cut out of the wood so the wind flowed through the whole fan. It was my favorite, and she didn't use it very often. I really hadn't ever discovered a pattern to why she brought it out sometimes. I was thinking about asking her, but she was worrying and going to stay on task. "You sure you didn't go with me and Carolyn?" she asked.

"I remember that," I said. "No, I was with Aunt Melinda and didn't go with you. It was my choice. I remember that you asked me over and over if I was sure that I wanted to go to Melinda's for another summer and skip the beach trip."

"Now I wish I'd have made you go," she said. "We went to Disney and everything."

"I saw the pictures when we went to Carolyn's for Thanksgiving or Christmas or something," I said. "When I saw those, I wished that I had gone, too, but I really did what I wanted to do at the time. There's no point in worrying about it now." I watched her fan move until it made me dizzy.

"You mean to tell me that you've never seen the ocean?" she said, her mouth drooping, as if the longer she considered it, the more she couldn't believe it was true. She slumped, and Miss Emy was never someone who slouched. "I feel so bad about that, Robin. I could've drove us to the beach one summer. I was so wrapped up—" she stopped herself.

"Have you heard from him?" I asked, knowing that she meant my dad.

"Yeah, Daniel called here yesterday," she said. "He said that he's out and back to working at that food pantry and shelter. Sounded like they're doing really good, and he's clean. I can always tell when he's clean, and he is. I believe he'll be alright this time." She paused and smiled, started her fan again. "I know that's who you meant. He asked about you."

"That's who *you* meant," I said.

She looked confused, but recalling her statement, pushed her fan toward my face in a big motion. "I'm sorry," she said.

"Ah," I said and waved my hand toward her.

"I am sorry that I never took you to see the ocean."

"It's alright. I understand, Miss Emy. I'm just excited to play music in different places."

She hugged me. "You have the best time," she said. "Don't you worry about nothing but having a good time." She stepped away from me with both of her arms straightened and her hands holding onto my arms so that she could look at me in full length. "You've earned this, and I think some really big things will come out of it." She took in a big breath and let go of me.

"I smell the biscuits," she said, crinkling her nose. "Oh, and I hear the gravy." The fragrance of the biscuits reminded me then of the solidity of the wood, the smell of carpentry, the stability of building in the home, in the kitchen. I heard the gravy splattering and popping under the lid, sputtering and bubbling with butter and was reminded of the music of the family, the group combining to blend into a perfect harmony.

That simplicity calmed my nerves as it always had. The biscuits and chocolate gravy were my comfort foods. As a child, they were a treat that brought me a sugar rush and a rich lingering of chocolate to savor, as Miss Emy always used pure cocoa. Another way for her to make it special, Miss Emy permitted me to use a lot of butter when eating that meal, too. Closing my eyes to smell and hear it with her then, her fan wafting the smell and memory of it, I knew that I had come for the magic, and I planned at that moment to dig up the spot where the metal detector had landed, beeping, all that time ago, no matter what she had to say about it.

When I told Miss Emy, she said, "I'll help you. If, you promise me that's the last you'll bring it up." She slowly waltzed the fan, a steady stroke of satisfaction for her clever deal.

We both knew the exact spot, and I surmised that she, too, had thought about it since the day Aunt Melinda interrupted us. I carried the metal detector out there to be sure, and it applauded our efforts. I jumped on the shovel and moved a pile of lemongrass and lamb's ear aside. The torn leaves sent a citrus signal out into the air, a casting fragrance of quilted leaves pulled apart. I half expected to see a yellowy poof, as it felt as if we'd opened the perfumed seal of a letter. After a few shovels, a deep thud sang out and through me. A bellows rang up through the wooden shaft and iron handle. Miss Emy and I looked at one another. She handed me the pick axe, and I dug out a wider hole, removing the bundle of lemongrass wound up with the tendrils of lamb's ear, as if it were the ribbon falling away from a tightly wrapped package. We saw the iron through the dirt. I pulled away parts of hydrangea roots, getting tighter underneath its branches, as the hole grew. I wiped away bits of dirt, and we could see a rounded iron dome. "Not very deeply buried after all," I said. "I'm doubting this is a trunk of treasure."

She swatted her fan for me to stop talking and continue digging. "This would beat all if that trunk was sitting here under their noses the whole time. They were running way off in the hollers and it was right here," Miss Emy said, as I continued to dig. Sunset was coming on strong. I slapped at the mosquitoes. Miss Emy whipped the fan into a frenzy and speculated. "It might not be anything but some old farm equipment or some part of the construction of the house that got abandoned over here."

"What a find," I muttered and wiped the sweat dripping into my eyes.

The lemon balm patch lay in between a row of hydrangeas and a few lilacs. "You can't hurt those," Miss Emy said, motioning for me to dig right into the lilacs. "They have always grown and bloomed like crazy. I just love the color, even if they take up a lot of space. Everybody says that they're delicate, but shoot, that's never been the case with these."

"I wish this one would get out of my way right now," I said, breaking a branch that kept poking me in the back while I tried to shovel out another part. "This might not be deep, but it's kicking my butt." I stopped and wiped my forehead with the hem of my t-shirt. "It better be worth it," I said looking down into the ground, threatening. "It's about to get dark, but I don't want to stop now. I can see the whole top of whatever it is."

"I'll run and get the lanterns," she said.

She returned twice. First, with two lanterns and next with freshly percolated coffee. I hugged her when she gave me the coffee and held my pick axe. After that, I was on a roll, removing enough dirt and breaking up the rest so that we could find "Handles!" I exclaimed. I tossed aside the pick axe for the shovel.

When we finally pulled it from the earth after a few tugs, and wiggled it back and forth, and pried it up from underneath with the shovel and our fingernails, the trunk was bigger than we thought. Later, we realized that it was quite a small iron trunk without a lock.

"If it had a lock, we'd be in trouble," she said. "We couldn't bust no iron locks off."

It was hard enough to pry open after being buried. We carried it onto the big table on the porch, leaving the lanterns and tools. My hands and arms ached, and I ate a spongy biscuit swiped in cold chocolate gravy while we worked on the lid. The whole time we anticipated what might be inside.

After an hour, we got the stubborn lid to finally lift. Both of us were afraid to look for a moment. I peered over it and sneezed. "Bless you," Miss Emy said and looked inside, too. We looked at one another and shrugged. She reached in and pulled out a piece of clear plastic holding something wrapped in cloth tied with twine. I gave her a quizzical look because it was plastic and a modern cloth, nothing from an indigenous tribe. She opened the cloth and revealed several books, small leather-bound books. When we opened the top one, a greeting awaited us from Ma Zona. "You have discovered the trunk of Arizona Ballard. I am burying it before I pass to the Great Mother. The person who carries on the tradition of hunting the treasure will know what to do..."

"Well, I'll say..." Miss Emy clucked, mouth agape, fan swishing.

"Can you believe this, Miss Emy?" I asked. "She believed in it the whole time. This was her trunk and it looks like she buried it in the 1960s."

"All that time," Miss Emy said. "She, too, had been searching for the treasure without telling anyone else." She breathed heavily. "Well, I'll say she must've been old when she buried this thing. Can you imagine?"

That notebook seemed to contain everything Zona knew about the treasure and where she had looked on the property. Miss Emy removed another bundle from the trunk. When she removed the cloth, a large deck of cards sat in her hands. She blinked, dropped them onto the table with a little toss as if they might be a poisonous thing, and slid her chair back quickly from the table. She shuddered. "Those," she said and got her fan going.

"Is it okay if I keep them, Miss Emy?" I asked, knowing immediately that they were Ma Zona's tarot cards.

"You can keep all of it," she said. "No, no, this is not for me. She meant this for her future family." She shook her fan nervously in front of her face and refused to touch anything else in the trunk. I lifted the covers of the other notebooks and peeked inside. From the trunk, I removed items all wrapped in plastic—a small quilt, a stack of quilt squares, a box with a turquoise ring set in silver, a necklace of opal and turquoise, a box of sewing needles and thimbles, one of spools of threads, a box with two small silver rings, one with coins, including a box filled with two-dollar bills, probably a hundred of them, and one last box with feathers that she identified with a list on top.

Miss Emy went to retrieve the lanterns "and whatever we left outside." I carried everything of Ma Zona's upstairs to my room, leaving the trunk on the table downstairs. Miss Emy lugged it up the stairs and nearly dropped it on my bedroom floor by the closet.

"I could've helped you with that," I said.

"I wanted to walk up here anyway," she said and opened her fan. She sat in the chair and closed her eyes behind the breeze she drummed up. After sighing heavily, she said, "I wanted to see you in your room. Like you used to be." She smiled and closed her eyes. It was after midnight, and the fatigue cloaked her body.

Suddenly, the kettle whistled loudly from downstairs. "Shoot," Miss Emy stood quickly and hurried out, saying, "I put it on for tea."

As I sat there looking over everything, Miss Emy was back in as quick a flash as she left. She carried big mugs of tea with tea balls bouncing inside of them and handed one to me. She sat in the chair and sipped at her tea. I smelled the steam rising out of my mug. "Chamomile," I said.

Miss Emy smiled. "It's from that batch last summer that we dried. Don't have much left."

"It has a strong fragrance," I said.

"Yeah, I like this one," she said. "Helps me sleep. The older I get seems the harder it is to get to sleep."

"I love you, Miss Emy," I said. "I'm glad we dug this up."

"I am, too," she said. "Not what I expected, but I reckon she left you some good things in there. That jewelry." She set her tea down and waved her fan in my direction. "No telling how old it is. Come from her family. She always wore those two little rings on her pinkie fingers. Maybe you'll find out why in one of them notebooks."

"I remember you telling me about the two rings when I interviewed you that time. I don't know if she'll say why, but one of these notebooks is about plants, from what I can tell so far. Looks like some kind of spells using plants and recipes," I laughed nervously.

"I don't doubt that a bit," Miss Emy said. "She was mysterious, you know. Some folks would say she was a witch. Like an old timey witch, an Indian one."

"It's Native Americans now, Miss Emy," I said.

"You know what I'm a-tryin' to say," she said. "She probably was one, a Native witch or whatever they were. They had a name for what they called them medicine people. I can't think of it right now. You've got me flustered that I'm gonna say it wrong."

"A shaman?" I asked.

"That's it." She smacked her hand against her fan. She nodded and smiled in the direction of the pile of Ma Zona's belongings on my bed. "If she hadn't buried all this..." Miss Emy trailed off, not finishing. "I'm tired," she said and picked up her unfinished tea. "I'm glad you're staying a couple of nights." She rose to leave. I knew that she had meant that my dad would have pawned all of these treasures or she, herself, probably would have gotten rid of them years ago. I certainly wouldn't have been sitting there with all of it had Ma Zona not buried the trunk.

"I love you, too," Miss Emy said, as she left the room. The meaning drifted in double, a love for me and for Ma Zona and her magic.

Sumac

Medicine for splendor in unbreakable friendship

Reliable as hide
Berries shine scarlet
For drawing out brightness,
For pretty coloring,
For sour lollies,
For flavoring powder,
For cool drinks together.

Seven | Ol' Time Tales & Trails

THE WHOLE STAY felt as if it was the beginning of a spiritual journey. I lay in my old bedroom thinking about it. My guitar was beside me on the bed, the first one that I had played, the one that I had used to win the Poke Sallet Festival Pageant. That guitar stayed close, and I felt proud of its birthmarks. Daddy figured out how to change the strings with me, carrying it half strung to the music store and questioning old Albert Wheeler until his eyes glazed over. Mr. Wheeler could play anything, and he taught me tricks every time I saw him. The instruments were the only possessions my daddy protected for me. That says something about him.

I was home, aware, and changed, knowing so much more than when I left for college, and not only the typical ways that people imagine and experience, but I was aware of my family's truths. I knew my great-grandmother, and no one else in my family knew her in the same, open way that I did. I had seen Cora spry again in her old age, and it seemed impossible and yet absolutely feasible at the same time.

Now, some of her mother's treasures surrounded me. Perhaps the shroud that covered Zona's past would be lifted in the process. I expected more books, photographs, documents, more confessions, as Hoot might have left if he had buried a trunk for the family. I wondered if maybe he had, but I thought better of it considering that I had most of his journals and notebooks.

Ma Zona's second notebook in the trunk was stained red leather. It appeared to be hand-dyed. The first plant was drawn in ink and accompanied with a poem and a kind of spell, a meaning. Wild Roses. *Medicine for long-awaited plans to fruit and long-kept secrets to be revealed.*

I certainly felt as if that was happening alright. The poem gave me a shudder. I looked up and around the room. The moonlight shone through the window, and I felt cold with knowing that she was aware that her treasure had been unearthed.

I drifted in and out of reading Ma Zona's notebooks. There was an inscription on the front page of one, in dark brown ink:

Zona Ballard. Delores Landry.
Ida Kessee. Cardy Headman.
1919 - 1939.
Our Sacred Covenant to the Earth's Medicine

Each name was signed by a different hand and each woman placed a period after her name. I didn't know these names, except maybe Delores. I thought that might be Ma Zona's sister. Someone mentioned her in the stories. I had to know who these women were and what their covenant could be. I flipped the page and settled into my pillows.

~ ~ ~

We aim to seal our rituals of protection and preservation. We were tasked with it, a ritual passed on from our mothers, a sacred duty from the ancestors, and there would be no denying it. I am passing it on here, to the one who discovers and reads this. A story of long efforts through the ages and many birth pains and death returning. I have lain down my efforts and won't pass this to my daughters. It blesses the land and future, yet it burdens the setter and the present. The past marches forward and makes it so, and I, for my part in the past will set the record down with the help of the writer, Cardy Headman. We will tell the story of the stone medicine made for all. Some of our people told legends, of portals and gateways to other worlds from the Great Spirit, through these, so our journeys took up the challenge of protecting them. There are sacred places, where the ancestors communed with the gods and goddesses, the creatures of the divine and spirit. And we journey to these places, for healing medicine and for connections between the Great Spirit and all that is between us and the earth. We have marked off the places for twenty years, just we four, continuing the process that was shaped long before us, and with the hope of preservation.

In ancient times, there was a Great Standing Stone that was the guide and marker. She oversaw everyone on the passage through the Valley. The stone was shaped as a cougar, the wild guardian of the lands. Ancestors met there and made decisions, all the ones from different areas from here to the ocean, to the west, to the north, to the mountains. They came together at the Great Standing Stone, every decade. They met and traded, made agreements and celebrations, became friends, maybe some became enemies.

Our Mama told us about the explosion. It was a blast that destroyed our Great Stone. She told me and Delores that they scattered the sacred stone with dynamite. The big cougar was high and rained down when they needed the space for train tracks. Mama gathered some pieces of the stone. She gave some to me and Delores. It is wrapped in the red bag. Mama told us about her Mama standing beneath the cougar stone, and she received a medicine that told her to "keep on going." That is what Delores and I do—we carry the vision into the future.

I am the anchor, pulling all sides of every stone down into the earth, seeing it attached by roots into the limestone, sandstone, clay, river stone. There are more than four sides to every rock, and we four represent all that blending of ancestors. It was passed down to me and Delores, the same teachings, even if we reflect our heritage differently. Delores is light and willowy.

Cardy is the marriage of French and British, and her Ma said they were part African and Iroquois, but she wasn't certain, just like the rest of us. Cardy has red hair. Her skin is light and creamy. I knew her Ma and she was African Islander, but very light. She was friends with my Mama when we lived at the ocean. That's how Cardy and her Ma came to live in Tennessee. They tethered to us.

"The tide pulls," Mama said. She was undone and went back to the ocean. She loved the water, and she felt freer, even if her people are from the woodlands. She mailed one letter, yet she stubbornly refused to tell more. Dada read everything, but he died in a train crash.

They wanted both of us to get schooling. Only Delores managed to go to Fisk, where she met and married her a doctor who graduated from Meharry. That Dr. Joseph Victor Landry wore small round glasses and kept a neat trimmed mustache. I embroidered handkerchiefs as a gift on his graduation day. He smiled at them in the afternoon sun. We all stood on a wide lawn for a photograph. After that, they moved with Mama to New Orleans, and she stayed hid away.

Delores gave me a lot of their books, even when Dr. Landry got mad about it. Mama emphasized my mastery of the material, even if I couldn't go to college. However it came to be, I can make something happen. People do my bidding. The earth responds to my requests. Every measure involves humility or nothing happens.

I took after Mama and had learned to bring babies into this world and help women screaming for relief. Mama understood how to soothe the Mama and pull out a baby at the right time. She held my face, said, "Two in this, Mama and baby. Always take care, Mama and baby."

My first Mama and baby, the Mama had lost two already with a doctor somewhere she lived previous. After the baby cried out and I gave the girl to her Mama, she kissed the baby girl to her face. She said, "Zona, you have the gift." Round about two or three months passed, and she come by to see me with her baby girl. She pressed two rings into my palm, "one for each hand, to remember, you have the gentle and the tough hands." I reckon I was sixteen, and I've been wearing the rings ever since.

We were little when Mama moved to our place in Tennessee, and folks was arguing about whether it was Tennessee or Kentucky sometimes. A long argument. Mama bought a house next door to Kessee's Funeral Parlor. I was infatuated with the horses in the barn. Kessee's kept black stallions, beautiful saddlebreds, that pulled a gleaming coach for some funerals. There was twenty acres fenced behind the funeral parlor and part of it went behind our house. I loved to watch the stallions graze in the field and I stood on the fence when the riders took them along the edges of the fence line and then out for a ride. Back then, people rode in town. There's a legend 'bout how old man Kessee got the first stallions, but I ain't a mind to tell it. Guess 'cause it's not mine to tell. Eventually, Kessee's replaced the stallions with motorcar hearses. They kept an old timey hearse displayed in the front circle driveway, and the stallions grazed in the back.

This was in the old time when folks went round in wagons and buggies. It sure was dusty and there's s'many flies, you couldn't hardly stand it in the summer. I met Ida right away. She was mooning over Benny Kessee, and she never stopped lurking at the funeral parlor. She carried a dolly, braided clover stems, always offered candies and bread to Benny, held Benny's hand as soon as he reached the end of his driveway, and said she was marrying him to become Mrs. Ida Kessee and have plenty of babies. That's what she did, but I swear she was born Mrs. Ida Kessee. Those babies didn't come right away, though they did eventually have children, dark black and beautiful, matching those stallions and hearses. Course I brought near every one of her babies into this world with her. She trusted me cause I never lost a Mama nor a baby. I sure did think I'd lose a few, but Bless my Soul, my Mama was with me, the Ancestors protecting over us all.

I don't get worried saying it or seeing it because Ida can talk to spirits and she knows the beginnings and the endings. That's her special talent, and Mama told me and Delores that the moment she met Ida sitting on the dirt path in front of the funeral parlor talking to herself and someone else invisible. Ida was braiding the stems of clover flowers. She wore a long pale pink dress, flowers embroidered at the hem and across the chest, flowing beautifully against her black skin. The clover braids looped around her legs and knees and lay in the folds of her dress.

"Talking to them spirits," Mama said to her.

"Telling me," Ida said.

"Remember." She nodded and kept going toward the store, while Delores, Cardy, and I stood in front of Ida staring. Delores sat down and began to braid.

"C'mon, Zona. Cardy," Mama called over her shoulder. I wanted a dress like Ida's with the delicate yellow roses and purple violets stitched on it.

"Delores?" I said.

"She's alright." Mama waved for us to follow.

Ida looked at Delores and whispered, "They tell me she'll bring us candy back."

"Who?" Delores asked.

"Ones you can't see," Ida said.

Cardy grabbed my hand and we followed after Mama. I didn't say anything about the candy comment. Mama bought a sour Indian lemonade for me and

Cardy, and we passed it back and forth until it was all gone by the time we made it back home. Mama gave Ida and Delores a big twist each, and I never even saw her ask for them in the store. I tried to recall the inside of the store. I always wanted the twists, especially when they were peppermint. I could tell by the look on Delores's face that they were.

Ida knew the art of listening. Maybe we all knew it, as she swore that we did, but Ida had always used the invisible more. She even directed it on us. Yet, she was correct about the places—even if we protected them with ritual medicine, not all of them would become as safe as we could make them. Some would be highly visible, and some would not, no matter how hard we tried.

Ida said it wouldn't be no use in trying for the Bluff Cave, even if we celebrated Emancipation Day there. That was where everyone went, so I was sure that it would never be forgotten. Mama said it was over a thousand people for it one year, but I swan ye to my time, if that cave didn't disappear. Ida said somebody told her they sold it, and somebody else said that it was filled in when they tore up the streetcar line and made the road round through there like it is now.

She said that we had to stick with the obvious places, and later when we got to the caves, we would choose one. The first obvious place was the great door of stone. All of our pathways traveled from there.

~ ~ ~

I couldn't believe it. I stopped reading, opened my bags, and pulled out Hoot's journals. I carried one of them around with me most of the time. I placed one of them next to Zona's and shuddered—both of them together. I couldn't help but wonder what was about to be revealed to me. So many questions passed through my mind—Did Hoot know about Zona's journals? This one that looked like a spell book? Did he understand what she was doing? Was he in on it? And then, all the questions about Great Aunt Cora rose up. Had she told me the truth? And why would I even think she lied about such a thing as being my great-grandma? Would Ma Zona confirm it all?

Ol' Time Tales
Lyrics by Robin Ballard

Gimme those ol' time tales and trails
And a jar of honeysuckle wine
Any old time. I'll ride those rails
To find a still of moonshine

In my dreams of the past
The spirits of my kind
Reveal the secrets that won't last.
On those ol' time trails
Where they sing the ol' time tales.

Amazing grace leads us to the place
For taking those switchbacks
Getting on track with the right pace.
Gimme those ol' time tales and trails...

~ ~ ~

Mourning
Lyrics by Robin Ballard

They said, "This invasive species must go."
She said, "Father, forgive them. They don't know
They just don't know."

They came to cut down the thistle
Render it useless and make the wind whistle.
Howling over the fields
Bawling through the years...

Sage

Medicine for to cleanse the space, to protect and encircle the sacred

Cleanse.
Run, Spirit of all.
Run, spirit to burn a wall.
A wafting wall of protection.
Furl, Spirit of purification.
Furl, spirit to mix a rub.
A savoring rub of satisfaction.
Crumble, Spirit of sensation.
Crumble, spirit to sprinkle a balm.
A benediction balm.

Eight | The Sweeper

TRACING MY HAND over the pages of Ma Zona's books, I marveled at her drawings of the flowers, her penmanship in neat cursive, and her need to tell the story of her life. The chamomile flowers were tinged with a spill that looked like coffee. I wondered where she sat while drawing and writing out each poem, and I tried to imagine her in different places throughout Miss Emy's house, *her* house first. Perhaps she sat in the medicine wheel. The page with sage was smudged with dirt. Here and there, she pressed the leaves and flowers in between the pages. How bright the purple sage blossoms remained flattened into the paper.

~ ~ ~

We don't say the names of our ancestors. We don't refer to ourselves as Indians. We don't talk about the rituals, the blessings, the way of the earth and sky, the stones and waters. I don't know enough, but I remember as much as Mama taught me. We all agree that we don't know enough. There were tribe women marrying white men. They didn't walk. They didn't go. They didn't pass on all of their traditions either. They didn't tell people their identities. I cannot understand how my Great-Grandma would feel, who she was so different than me.

Except I know from Nenny about the old ways. She's Hoot's Ma, and she takes my hand and reminds me. The first time she led me to the cave, I could not accept that it was true. I married into my heritage without knowing it all the way. As my Mama said, "It will never sleep. We will never blend all the way into white pages." She thought that idea was "too flat," and she often smacked her hands together. "We believe in this," she told me and Delores. She picked up a handful of dirt and the brown grains fell through her fingers, some stones and rocks remained in her palms, some shone and reflected light. She taught me the ways and I honor her requests.

We are guided by the moon and her changing faces. After the new moon is the time to go and complete the protections. Before the full moon, we make our way home. Straying from this invites danger. Clip the herbs and plants above the earth when the moon has been past dark more than two days. The sliver of her curling hair is there. Cutting the herbs and plants, and anything above the earth after the moon is full brings its decline and recession. Pulling the roots and trimming after the moon is full blesses the stock, the trunk, for the future. Peeling the bark when the moon is full offers the most potency.

We traveled carefully every time the four of us met. I was often the last to arrive, but I was bringing the mystical ones. Most people cannot believe, so it's better not to discuss the deer serpent undulating the ground and the dragon rabbit bounding through the treetops. Instead, I arrived at the door of stone with beings unseen. I rode Gala, my buckskin quarter horse, and we were accompanied by Blue and Goldie, my bugle mouth hound and a large yellow cur that guarded well. Delores traveled alone, taking trains and coaches. Sometimes, when she visited me before our journeys, she rode Glider, our bay quarter horse. Cardy and Ida made the journeys together, changing it up from riding, Ida on Coffee and Cardy on Rufous, to trains and even to a motorcar in the end. None of us ever backed out.

We could depend on our jobs, helping women to birth babies and aiding in burials, as a cover for activities—being four women traveling alone together and meeting up in the woods. Mostly though, no one bothered with knowing that we met. There was nothing much to hide even if we thought that we needed to be sneaky. It was more scandalous that I was leaving my family to fend for themselves while I went off to cast protections on places that my ancestors believe are special.

A baby was always being born, so services were needed. Mrs. Greeter delivered a baby out there unexpectedly. We heard her screaming, and Delores followed the sound. She popped her head into the kitchen window and shouted, "This is Delores! We're here to help you."

We all laughed. Ida said, "Oh, she feels relieved now, as if you're the Blessed Virgin Mary."

She did open the door, still crying and yelling, saying, "I'm Mrs. Greeter," in between. She explained that the doctor couldn't be reached. Her husband left her alone and went to find a midwife or somebody to help her, and she just lay there hollering. She hadn't seen a doctor or no one the whole time she was with child. We got her all set and was delivering the baby when her husband came back with a doctor. That crazy *husband called us witches and accused us of wanting her baby. "We don't need none of your jaw," Cardy hollered back. "We're a-trying to help your wife!"*

That husband picked up a broom and come after us, and we had to run through the woods. Cardy got lost and ended up on a farm down the road. That was the biggest calamity we got into in the beginning. They told us that Mrs. Greeter named her baby Delores.

The great door of stone spoiled us by thinking it would all go so easily. Cardy's family lived near there, so we had a place to stay, even if it was her Mamaw's old stinking cabin that smelled of goats. On my way, Gala worked up lather even though the sun was going down. It was nearing the summer solstice, and we kept the plan as our mothers had told us.

The Plan

The great door of stone protection round, up and down,
Set the medicine ritual, First.
Move through the arches, sew the twins together
south and north,
buffalo turn the passageways, Second.
Circle round the mushroom
up high and seal the reverence
with a shared drink, Third.
Float under the waterfalls
that creek and fall,
that scale and fall
behind the moonbow falls, Fourth.
Hold hands and snake
through the underworld
with your sisters and sing

together there, all the songs
we have not taught you, Fifth.
Wind along the river
in the water,
up the mound,
humming and laughing,
recalling each place, each blessing,
and leaving, Sixth.

> *Initial*
> *Delores*
> *Sweep, sweep. Sage*
> *And treat the weeping willow*
> *Billow, billow, feather sweep,*
> *Sweep, sage and smoke.*

Delores arrived with her sage brooms. All spring and summer the year before, the sage grew until Delores clipped it with large silver scissors that slice and gleam. She tied the stems in red-purple string, pokeberry dyed strands, and hung the sage in the cellar. The silvery plant's tiny purple flowers were soft but sent a fragrance of rubbed wood, the agitated pungency of bark that's being bothered. The bundles hung nearly to the ground. In the winter, she bound them into brooms.

At the great door, she found a rough passage of stone ascending between two bluffs. A rocky cedar ridge met a sandy ridge dotted with pines. Delores was alone and carried two brooms. With the willow and sweet grass bundle, she swept each step up. At the top, she walked the stone and swept a circle that the wind shook up. She struck a match and lit one end of the sage broom. *The smoke drifted over the treetops in the valley. She sang out her blessing.*

Ida Kessee brought the feather, a robin's feather, simple and everywhere, she said. Her blessings were that our protections would be simple and bless humankind. Ida sprinkled her powders, probably herbs, old papers, and bones. She knew bones and bodies, the visible and invisible.

When I arrived, the prophecy came to me before I saw any sights. I heard Delores's voice and I could see the girl, a granddaughter, singer as a bird. That was my contribution, the blessings of prophecy and birth.

We held hands and walked the length of the stone, up and down, many times, humming a new melody without words.

Eventually, Cardy Headman offered her words, which are always needed, for the powers of existence respond to marked phrases spoken in time.

"May this passage be a door to all in the future and may all protect its sacred wild lands and feel a sense of wonder and responsibility to fulfill this blessing. We four witness this medicine of protection and preservation into existence."

We were soaked in sweat, and the wind at the top of the ridge slipped over us as if we had slid into the cool of the creek. Cardy and I walked back a little stretch to where we left the horses. Gala and my dogs were under a piece of quilt and hide I hung up. We walked about a half a mile to the creek and got more water for them, fed them what we brought from home. I took out my sleeping roll. We decided not to go back to Cardy's Mamaw's cabin.

By the time we got back to the campsite with the supplies, Ida's fire welcomed us. She made tea, and I fell asleep looking at those stars before I even finished my drink.

~ ~ ~

Reading the words of Ma Zona's journal did not feel real. The whole series of events felt like a dream to me. Miss Emy and I had dug a hole in the medicine wheel and found Ma Zona's buried trunk, not the treasure that everyone was sure existed out there, but a treasure to me because of what this was telling me.

I couldn't help but understand it as more than a coincidence, and my mind was going more than a little crazy. I was sure that Ma Zona was referring to the same place that Kevin and I went to, where we played music on the cliff that day. Then again, *there could be other stone stairs in a bluff, right? Had she prophesied my existence when she mentioned a girl, granddaughter, singer as a bird? How does that happen? It was 1919. What did I have to do with that place? I was born nearly seventy years later. And, I was her great-great-granddaughter, not a granddaughter. Would Kevin believe this? Would anyone? Was I putting too much together that didn't go together?*

I read it again and again, just to be sure it was there and to try to resolve some of the questions in my mind. Yet, more questions grew.

I didn't want to tell anyone else, not yet. I didn't know why but I wanted to protect these revelations and the whole *digging-up-the-trunk-in-the-yard* thing.

Bearberry

Medicine for dependability

You need to eat,
You need to make a sweet,
You need a smoking mixture,
You need texture,
You need yellow color,
You need fruit flour,
Bearberry
Many names
Mountain cranberry
Many uses
Fox plum
Many admirers
Born in sand
Hog Craneberry
Devil's tobacco
Mealberry
Kinnikinnick

Nine | Sisters Sewing

WHERE IS THERE a garden and a stone, a settlement in the middle of sandstone? I woke up with this question on my mind after reading more of Ma Zona's notebooks.

~ ~ ~

Mixture
Zona
Of feather and claw
Of hide and law,
Of fur and rugged silver smoothed
Ragged to shine
A rough rare wildling
Birthed in the garden
Breathing in the roses'
Forever spells
In blooming
Disguises.

In 1920, when we went to the needle and its arches, we stayed in the town of No Business. Hoot had a cousin on Nenny's side of the family, and she wound up over there in the wild lands. Her family was there way back on account of her great-great-grandfather serving in the War with the man that formed up the settlement.

This sequence of protections would take us a week to complete. Each sandstone rock was out in the wilderness and separated many miles from one another. We planned to forage for bearberry, birthroot, and other herbs and mushrooms to aid in childbirth and menses, and for the itch folks get from rubbing up against each other—that would have to do as our excuse for wandering the woods alone. To get to slippery elm, we sought places that escaped the destruction of bark hunters. Cousin Litton and the folks at No Business were helpful in directing us where to find plants. "There's a springhouse left down there close to Charity Creek. If you camp there, you'uns can use it," Cousin Litton said.

We all knew that Cardy had her a hunter and a miner out there. One was salt mining in them rocks, and the other was on another side of the forest living and hunting. She had men all over, and I don't know what she said to keep herself free, yet her way with the honeyed tongue must have been convincing and smooth.

"They aren't wanting to keep me," she joked when we teased her about it. "I choose men who don't require collections."

"Hmmm," Ida smirked. "That's because you're the collector. A mantis."

"Hussy," Delores said.

"I am," Cardy laughed. "'Cept I leave their heads on to love another day."

Delores fanned her broom out around in a circle, as if protecting herself from the consequences of Cardy's escapades. "I don't know why all those men appeal to you."

Cardy closed her eyes and breathed deeply. She put her hands up in front of her chest, reaching out her fingers, "Taut bodies." She smiled a wide grin and opened her eyes. "I'm light as one of your brooms compared to what they do."

"MmmMmmMmmm," Ida said. "Aren't you?"

The eye of the needle made from sandstone watched us. We approached down a long sliver of trail, a pale rusty depression in the earth, stretched out beneath dark trees. Blue bayed at the eye, as if it were an animal or some type of living thing. Goldie growled to show her agreement. The arch looked small from the distance, and by the time we got there, I felt inspected by this giant eye of the forest, a gateway recognized by ancestors. A shag bark hickory grew through the side of the needle's eye.

"Zona, how did Mama know about this?" Delores asked me as we tied the horses.

"Stories," I said. We fed and watered the animals, then stood in front of the needle, staring at it.

Ida bowed slightly as before a temple and then walked up onto the sandstone. She scrambled up the stone quickly, as if she were ascending a staircase, rolled out her blanket on a sliver of the needle and lay down.

Delores pulled two small brooms from her bag. Carefully, she swept the ground with the sweet grass and tobacco bundle. She hummed underneath it. She set the sage broom on fire, blew it out so that it would smoke, and held it with the other broom against her side using her elbow. Then, she used her other hand to leverage against the hickory piercing the eye and climbed onto the arch. Once she was up there, Delores placed the sage broom down on top of the arch. The smoke drifted with the wind down the path we had just traveled to get there. Delores continued to sweep, the top of the needle this time, with her sweet grass bundle, moving all around Ida, humming and asking for protection in a muttering rhythm.

"You ready?" Ida sat up and asked me. She made up our kinnikinnick, a smoking mixture from bearberry, mullein, and sumac. She motioned for me to climb up.

On the arch, I pulled out the quilt squares, the needle and thread, from my bag. I had wild vanilla, what we called deer's tongue, and Ida added that to our smoking medicine. We changed it, depending on what we had. Dogwood, sassafras, devil's thornapple seeds, blackberry and strawberry leaves. The blend was whatever we carried, for the plants have to be dried first.

Cardy was setting the fire for camp. She searched for food. "I'm hungry," she told us a few times. I brought plenty of extra food, yet I wasn't telling Cardy until we were set up for the night. We all knew that she was pregnant and that the baby would not live. Cardy told us as much.

Ida and I started the sewing of the quilt. Mama gave me the cloths. Ida's Mama gave her some, too. I thought about our Mamas' embroidery work, as we pieced the fabric together based on the colors. Ida shrugged, "I don't know if this is the way it's supposed to go."

Humming, Delores joined us. "When Mama gave me these squares, she said, 'Any way you connect may offer a new route.' She said something else, but that's all I remember."

Cardy plopped down. "Camp's all set up, and I've got my squares, too. But I can't focus to sew with this gnawing in my stomach right now."

"I've got everything you need," I said to Cardy while we stitched our squares together.

"I know, but I don't see how it's supposed to do anything." She laughed, but it wasn't from humor.

"You don't have to be afraid," Delores told her. "You got yourself into this. You asked us for a way to change it."

"I don't understand," Cardy said.

"Some plants and barks, slippery elm and others," I said. "They'll do the work. You'll feel some pressure akin to getting your moons, possibly a bigger one."

She shook her head in agreement and sewed when Ida passed her a square. Delores circled us all with her sage broom.

"Shhh, you hear that?" Ida asked, motioning for us to be quiet. Blue whined. Seemed like one of the horses was uneasy. I grunted "no."

"Shhh, you think anybody's out here?" she asked.

"No," I said. "It's just the animals. People wouldn't like the looks of us anyway." I smiled.

Ida glared at me.

"You're hearing the spirits is all," I said to her.

"No, this was a route for those escaping, but it's not them. Keep thinking I hear men talkin'."

"I got something for 'em if they try anything," Delores said.

I heard Goldie growl. "You're getting the dogs worked up," I said.

We were all afraid of other people harming us, telling us to go away, following us, and other nightmares. Delores carried a gun and a sheath knife in her boot. Ida had a gun all the time. All of us carried a knife of some sort. A cased knife could do some harm if necessary. I had this little axe that we used to cut through parts of the trace that were overgrown.

"Got more than one thing," Cardy laughed. "My huntsman and my miner might be out there."

"I won't be depending on that," Delores said. "Some of these people scare me."

"I don't have any reason to be afraid of the folks out here, just trying to survive," I said.

"You're right," Ida said. "It's time to focus on the medicine." We shared the kinnikinnick from a pipe as we sewed, as we sang to the ancestors.

Late that night, we climbed down and slept on rolls. Above us, we suspended hides on ropes between the trees to keep us dry and warmer. As I placed my head down, I noticed a blooming trillium just aways from us. My eye caught a few more, speckled there, as if flickering out in the dark. At dawn, I opened my eyes to the sight of the wake-robin again, still there. I made a prayer and picked it, knowing the high probability that the plant would die or wait near seven years before flowering again among its kin.

Cardy never showed distress, but the next morning we knew all had come to pass without a word or symbolic deed from her. It was felt between us, and I believe that they, too, did an individual ritual for the passing, for honoring Cardy's decision.

Our promise was to focus on the preservation of the places. We packed up the camp and headed for the twins and on to the buffalo.

Blackberries

Medicine for to protect the traveler, to warn the wanderer in the wild

Guard! Call to the edge.
Crossroads of the quest
Where cicadas rattle.
Weigher of courage.
Blessed fruit of the strangled spot.
Great teacher of allure
And nourishment after danger.
The satisfaction of return
Is discovered in the memories
You offer each year. Markers of the pilgrimage.
Denizen of dessert
For rabbits, mice, birds, the deer.
Hideout for all, the honeybee
And the spider. Halt all who pass.
Halt for pleasure, for awareness and safety,
For satiety.
Halt, or the hooks will stop you.

Ten | One Long Song

THERE HE WAS, just like that. Ma Zona wrote about my great-grandfather, Harold Flynn. Out of nowhere, she wrote a page. She hadn't even written about her daughters or her sons for that matter.

~ ~ ~

Harold Flynn

He was a loner, but didn't nobody let him alone. He's one of those people that showed up with somebody and caused you to say, "I didn't know you knew Harold Flynn." Harold said in his own head that he hadn't known it either, but near everybody noticed him.

~ ~ ~

That was it. Nothing on the other side of the page. One page, so far. No mention of Cora or the baby or the letters. I wanted to skip through, but I made myself wait. Just wait.

~ ~ ~

Wind pierced the large and small arches, barreling down the paths as we crossed Charity Creek, far away from the laurel forks. I found the springhouse, near enough after crossing the main branch. I saw the tracks there, too. We knew the presence of animals. They weren't fond of getting close to humans.

In the rock houses, we collected snakeroot, sandwort, mullein, more bearberry and deer's tongue. Ida suggested that we make camp and let the animals rest before we picked our way through the huckleberry and laurel.

I expected the twins to be similar to the needle. Yet, my oh my, they stretched into the Heavens, the largest rocks I ever seen. I lay down underneath one of the twins, looking into the pines, maple, and blackgums, noticing that curve of earth jutting up into the sky, listening. A round of robins flitted under them.

We climbed up onto the top of one, finding a narrow, rocky crag to scoot up in places. From the top, we looked over the ridges, clear across the valley. Those twins were joined up top. I cried there, the sun on my face, the warm stone streaked with colors. We all wept as we descended the arches before the sunset. When Cardy began singing, I had never heard the song. Ida said, "It's from the future."

> *Below the arches, the robin sings*
> *A simple flight into backyard springs*
> *Me and you, I do.*
> *Me and you, we do.*
> *Stay true to the songs we sing*
> *And this backyard spring*

~ ~ ~

I slammed the book shut. Too much. No, it wasn't exactly our songs, but there were pieces of the songs in their song. In a buried journal. I had to ask myself if it was possible to catch glimpses of the future like that? The way we see little parts of the past so clearly sometimes?

I wanted to share this with Kevin, especially since he took me to these places. They seemed like the same places to me anyway, so I took a deep breath and told Miss Emy I'd be back after Atlanta. I packed up the backpacks, my clothes for the trip, guitar, mandolin, shoved it all in the car, and I took the whole drive to prepare my speech and display of evidence to Kevin.

"Intense," he said. "This is all a little more than overwhelming." He shrugged and handed the book back to me. He blushed and shuffled his feet nervously. He told me that he was headed out to the grocery store.

"Really?" I asked, confused by his odd response. When I was on my way to his house, I thought it was exciting. Maybe I was too eager in my delivery.

"What did you say exactly?" Angie asked me when I showed up and flipped out about scaring Kevin and possibly ruining the band. "I doubt you ruined anything," she said. We sat outside at the coffee shop where she worked downtown. She took a break after bringing me a tea and sat down beside me.

"I told him that I thought this was a sign about our possible success as a band."

"Ah, this is classic. Guy is afraid of the real deal behavior," she said.

"I'm not following you." I blew into the tea and took a sip.

"He feels guilty because he can't go to Atlanta with us, and I think he has a crush on you. You've brought him this message from the beyond or something, the real deal, and he got scared, felt guilty, all that. You know?"

"I never would have gotten all that," I said dropping my head in my hands.

"Don't worry. He'll call you anytime and want to know more about it."

"He will?" I asked.

"Yeah, unless he is a block of stone himself," she said. "And I know him a little more than you. He seems too curious to let something like this go. Where's the next place your grandma goes anyway? Have the two of you visited it?"

"I haven't gotten that far," I said. "It is *crazy* that we've been to the first two places, right? Or, places that are eerily similar?"

Angie pushed me. "Yes, they *are* those places! Where else would they be? Completely crazy." She picked up my tea and took a drink, then handed it back to me.

"I can't believe these journals," I said.

"Do you have them with you?" she asked.

I nodded. She flipped her palm open toward me. "Well, let's find out where the next place is."

~ ~ ~

Folks think of protection as a spell and that there are immediate results, as if a potion can be made and with a "voila" reveal dramatic differences. We know the flow of spirit is a richer depth and a lingering beyond our concept of time. It lasts the course of a lifetime—a song, a blessing, a medicine, maybe a curse—powerful. The very best of the accumulation of singing and playing, a receptive combination to the sounds of the time and the world, of the spirit. A riddle of decisions permeable as to become a tune that everyone knows, as if some Divine Truth is spoken in the songs. The communal love of a song could last centuries, building a family to be remembered.

That's how it came to be that I pushed out Harold Flynn so that the granddaughter will eventually live. She will have the great quest, and it's the only way to protect us all and our beliefs and songs. This is the way and you, you girl, you have been promised from the future as a blessing, from a prophesy that contained many blessings because we circumvented the curse. Ida Kessee helped to prevent a prophesy coming true. The yearning will be appeased, controlled and deliberate, a constant sewing of crying holy songs and stories.

You will be simple as a robin, a lovely brown,
Chestnut lover and watcher.
Blooming, you will become a beloved songbird
Birthed from the blackberry patch and lifted
By the Bluebird to the stage,
Surrounded by many singers
Accompanying your song.

We saw the woods runner tear through the forest as though she was dancing. Dewy gemmed spider webs hung across her chest, draped as a glittering scarf, a fringed dress with small leaves and seeds, flower petals, dirt and bark embroidered throughout. We stood over a robin's egg and received the prophesy.

"Bear," she said, eyes wide, veins straining, teeth gleaming in a smile. We stopped briefly. I gave her a bundle of huckleberries from a thicket we passed

earlier. She gave me a horseshoe and a robin's feather. She continued on along the trace.

"A shoe," Ida said lifting an eyebrow.

"Another robin feather," Cardy said.

"We're getting someone's story," Delores said. Cardy hummed an upbeat tune. Delores rode up next to Cardy and linked arms and joined her.

Ida rode Coffee close to me and Gala. I leaned so that our shoulders touched. "What do you think our Mamas knew about this?" she whispered. I shrugged and tried to stay in step with Cardy and Delores, but Ida pulled back. "I'm concerned it doesn't mean anything."

I gave her a quizzical look. I felt saddened by her question. "Why are we out here doing this?" she asked.

I stopped. "You know why," I said.

"I've forgotten," she said. "The source of it all."

"Our Mamas gave us this task. To visit these sacred places. Your Mama said that we needed to all be different but connected. Different relatives. Different talents. Different ancestors." She nodded, remembering.

Ida's face was dark and smooth as black marble, and she became serene. Her wise eyes closed for a moment. She took in a deep breath. "Yes, I remember."

"Do you think you're getting those?"

"Not yet," she said. "These messages have been for you. Descendents of Cora."

I thought so, too. Cora and Jane were already teenagers, and I worried about leaving them. Yet, the farm needed their care while I was away. "We're all getting parts of our stories, but it's not easy to sew together."

Mulberries

Medicine for finding strength in vulnerability and combining your strength with others

Versatile
Until you take it from the tree,
And it sweats and waits

A washing, a decision,
An instant before fingertips pluck
Them up and plop them for
The tang, the juice and crunch.
Versatile
Until waiting

On the counter
Drying in a towel, dripping softly,
The sweetness seeping into the fabric.
Melding
A mush into the bowl

Eleven | Full Circle Gospel

I WAS BEGINNING to live a future for myself that was more long term. I found myself in a state of surprise over and over that summer. I didn't think I would ever stop marveling at the world, how it changed and revealed more, and with my own self within it.

I listened to Angie all the same when she wanted to get advice and vent about her "life's unique challenges," as she was influencing me to say and to understand as a point of approach. I was trying not only to have one, but to *be* a good friend.

She was equally enraptured by plants. She admitted that was part of her allure to the band—that we sang about plants and wrote songs around them. The allure of plants is contagious, and I've come to understand our desire to maintain a sacred reverence for the work of soil and root.

Atlanta-bound, we were in the back of Martin's dad's van. He let us borrow it for some of our road trips. Martin was driving, and slowed down, while Angie and I blabbed about tea blends since she worked at so many restaurants and coffee places over the years. Even though they didn't always have names related to teas, it was understood that some of the drinks she served might have a special brew or blend, an interesting twist for the tisane drinker of a serious nature. She was getting into my project, explaining a blend. I looked out the window of the van. Slowing, cars and semis sped by us on the interstate's other side. I tried angling myself to see what was happening.

I eyed Martin through the rearview mirror. He wasn't saying anything. He rolled down his window. The scenery went by quickly. I couldn't see what the issue was. Martin slowed the van to a stop, but Angie kept talking, wrapped up in her story. Someone outside the van came into view. Martin seemed to smile at the man's form as he got larger. He turned his head as we stopped, rolled forward a little, stopped again. I shrugged toward Angie as if she might know what was going on. We were used to Kevin being with us, in the passenger seat, but without him, we were unaccustomed to asking Martin about his driving.

Angie asked, "What's going on?" because she could see the man now, too. He had a backpack. There wasn't a car.

"Need a ride?" Martin asked, looking out his window. The man glanced in. "We're headed to Atlanta, can take you that far if you're trustworthy."

"Honest," the apparent hitchhiker said. "Sounds good. Mighty appreciative."

"Martin!" Angie whisper-shouted. "What? Why would you do that? Do you know him?"

"He's fine. I can tell," Martin said as he rolled up his window and the man crossed in front of the van.

"You don't know him!" Angie declared. She wouldn't look at me and glared at Martin through the rearview mirror.

The man seemed to hesitate by the front of the passenger side door. Martin rolled down the passenger side window and said, "You can ride in the passenger seat."

The man glanced into the back seat when he put his backpack down in the floorboard toward the middle console. "Much obliged," he said and tipped his ball cap toward us, practicing his friendly face. "I didn't know which door, so I'm glad you told me."

Martin gave a quick glance through the rearview mirror to cue that he had read the signals from the man correctly. The subtle trust. Angie and I said an unspoken "okay" back to Martin. The eyes told all those stories.

The hitchhiker was probably thirty, maybe more, and something was easy and calm about him. "Needing a ride was all," he said. "I was afraid that I might have to survive off those shriveling mulberries back there by the side of the road. They're almost done."

"Mulberries?" Martin asked. "Those are real? Like in the song?" He sang "around the mulberry bush," and the hitchhiker laughed.

"Yeah, they're real." He opened his palm and revealed some shriveled mulberries already staining a circle in the center. "They're delicious, but I been a cowbird all my life, so course I think so."

I jumped thinking about Daddy saying those words on that trip so long ago. When Martin inquired what he meant, I felt like déjà vu was controlling my life, and I just froze up while he was talking about the habits of cowbirds.

"Friend of mine came up with it," he said.

Martin asked him the standard question, "So, where're you headed?"

"The beach," he answered with a sigh of contentment.

"Sounds like you're already seeing it in your mind," Martin said.

"Gotta visualize it before you can live it," he said.

"That's deep," Martin said. "Which beach?"

"Any beach," he said. "First one I can get to and then I'm going to keep going all the way."

"You mean to the tip of Florida?"

"Maybe, or in the other direction. Louisiana, Texas." He shrugged. "Mexico."

"I'd go for Florida," Martin said, "And just curve around and head up the whole east coast."

"Sure, you would," Angie said. "In a car. You've never walked more than across campus to class. Can you imagine walking in the sand for more than thirty minutes? Your legs would be screaming in pain."

"Is walking in the sand that tough?" I asked.

"You never been to the beach before?" Martin asked.

My face turned bright red, and I imagined they thought my whole family burned at the neck like that. I shrugged.

"Really?" he asked. I didn't know why but I almost cried and talked myself out of it, looking out the window, watching the cars pass.

"Never seen the ocean?" Martin asked. "It's okay," he said. "I mean it's not okay that you've never seen the ocean because I think you'll love it. Everyone does. And, we're going. I'm taking you." He made a declaration and nodded it into the rearview mirror.

"We have a show," Angie said.

"Not right now," he said, and looked over to the hitchhiker, "Sorry, man. We can't go right now." Then, back through the rearview mirror again, he added, "I meant later, but we're going." He smiled to me.

"You nervous about playing with the fiddler that I set us up with?" Angie asked me, referring to the fact that Kevin wasn't going along with us.

"Only when it comes to our own songs, and we just have four of those right now," I said. "He's a great musician. I like The Patch Brothers."

"Yeah, I hate doing the cover thing, too, but what choice do we have until we finish up more of our own songs?" She pulled at the ends of her hair framing her face. "The Patch Brothers are okay. I don't dislike them, but Martin and I met them a long time ago and he's not a fan. I like what you and Kevin have been coming up with."

I nodded. "You and Martin met them?"

"Yeah, four years ago, something like that, at a song writing camp for teenagers," she laughed.

Martin stuck out his tongue. "The Patch Brothers?" he smiled to Angie in the rearview mirror. "They think they are all that." He looked over to the hitchhiker. "You ever heard of them?"

"Nah," he said. " Don't think so, but I'd have to hear their music to know."

Martin launched into their most popular song. After the chorus, he stopped.

"Never heard it," the man said. He turned and looked back at me. "You'll blow him away, and he'll be the one who's nervous."

"That's right," Martin said, beaming.

We let the cowbird out when we got to Atlanta, and I never asked him if he was someone who knew my daddy or one of those teenage boys who hitched with us, but I wish now that I had asked.

And, he was right on. Both Patch Brothers were speechless. They couldn't agree on who was supposed to play with us. "Why don't you both play with us?" Angie suggested.

"That's what they were getting at anyway," Martin whispered to me. He was fuming. "They're trying to steal our part of the show."

We were in a big festival line-up. I had no idea how many bands were playing, and I hadn't ever heard of half of them.

I didn't bumble at all when we went onto the stage. I played one of my best shows, and those Patch Brothers got so messed up that they exited the stage after the second song. I had to make a joke on their behalf to pretend that their messing up was an act, same as I had to do for myself so long ago when I first started performing. I winked at Martin. He was thrilled when we continued for three more songs without them.

I think the crowd was most surprised by our cover of "Katie Cruel." It's always been a favorite of mine, and to turn it blue with Angie made my heart melt on the stage. We finished up with a gospel hymn that followed us around for the rest of the trip.

Martin kept his promise of taking me to see the ocean. When I saw it a few days later, the ocean exposed me—I felt vulnerable and afraid. The pervasive sound, the force of sun and wind, the stubborn shifting difficulty of sand, the smallness of accumulated power in all of these vast forms took my breath and flung it out to the horizon. I sat down on the shoreline and waited for my breath to return. I sobbed, and Martin and Angie thought it was for witnessing beauty, but it was for sensing the smallness of my existence next to the relentlessness of time. The ocean was a mysterious chasm, the tip edge of a mountain overlook, where lovers leap, where fog and foam, the cream of air and the froth of water, blanket all that lives in the dark, but it suddenly parts each instant to reveal ever more space, ever more mystery.

Martin sang, "And we shall meet on that beautiful shore."

Angie joined in, "In the sweet..."

And I sang, too, "In the sweet, by and by..."

Full Circle Gospel
Lyrics by Robin Ballard and Martin Paxton

The light shone in through the windows
And framed my grandma's face in double halos.
She hummed her songs to the Lord
And ran her fingers over the words.
Holding onto those holy tunes
She sang in the garden, full of blooms.
Her voice lifted high when she swept
And shined her house as a treasure she kept.
My Daddy said, "She sang them songs to me,
And her voice is still pretty as you please."
It's a full circle hymn, a family to grow
"Beee-bitty-bye-oh-baby-oh.
Beee-bitty-bye-oh-baby-oh."

Bee balm

Medicine for attraction and beauty, a clear voice

Monarda, you, sound...
Whispering your name is the sound
of lovers. Cooling fevers.
Hummingbird arrives, relieving the
stuttering of hearts over so many
tongues and mouths opening
to flicker feelers, collect
the horsemint. "You can eat
the leaves," someone says. "The flowers."
I laugh with knowing,
With clear breathing,
"Of course, you can."

Twelve | Buffalo Siren's Song

~ ~ ~

Listener
Ida
Quiet sister
Question sister
Dust sister
Flutter sister
Hands clasp
Healing sister
Roots sister
Bone sister
Seeing sister

THE MONARDA LINED the trace. "*Buffalo carved out the original way,*" *Ida said and pinched the flowers, placing them on her tongue until they dissolved. The flowers glowed a pale purple in the afternoon. Some were bleached white from the sun. "They say if you fall asleep out here at the buffalo arch, your dreams will prophesy the future.*"

"*Who told you that?*" *Cardy asked.*

"*Mama never said that,*" *Delores said, raising her eyebrow at me. "Did you ever hear tell of that?*"

"Naw," I said. "Mama didn't say nothing about it. Did you hear it from your Ma?" I asked Ida.

"I can't remember which one told me," she said, flicking her fingernails one by one with her thumbnail, recounting something in her mind. She made too many lists—all colors, buckets, titles, tasks to be completed, birthdays to be remembered, years and dates, plans of a lifetime in one day. Recommendations—books, songs, places. Pictures to go with everything. Drawings to remember. Documents to pass down so that someone remembers. Hammering out the records. She tapped her fingernails to the beat of soft harmonies.

The harmonica drifted through the forest folds—at times, it was louder and others it lingered. We were getting closer to it. We didn't speak and barely breathed. It began faintly and we might have left it alone. We might have sent only two, and two of us remained behind at the camp with the animals, the food, the provisions. Instead, I commanded only Goldie to stay. The song came louder so swiftly after the first curve that we all found ourselves playfully following it in afternoon light at first. Blue led the way. Ida whispered, "I think it's Benny. He's come to surprise us."

The trickle of musical notes tickled all of our curiosities and delighted us so that we became caught up in the belief that we'd certainly see the musician at any moment. Benny did play the harmonica and they didn't have no children then or farming to hold him back. If nobody died and he didn't have a funeral to attend to, then he could do as he pleased with his time. However, to think of him alone venturing out to find us, I was lost to create a picture of that in my mind.

The sound of the music retreated, drifted away, then paused. We waited, and Blue was silent. He whined and the song lured us again, saying don't linger too long. Soon, we were deep in the hollow. The sunset light that was in front of us tricked us into believing that the shadow wasn't behind us all the time. The darkness overtook us and our search until I stopped abruptly. "It's become dark. Look back, we'll never find the way now."

Clouds covered the light of the moon, if there had been any light, and shadows raced under the cloud cover. Cardy struck a match and lit the end of a mullein stalk. I always carried cedar pitch in case we didn't have a way to make a fire. I put some on the end of another mullein stalk and gave it to Delores. We were relieved to have those two golden torches.

"How far have we gone?" Cardy asked.

"We followed the creek for a while, so let's go back that way," Delores said, pointing the torch toward the way she wanted to go.

Blue started back. I heard Goldie bark in the distance. I paused and tried to sharpen my hearing. Goldie howled and bawled out about the time that other sounds picked up in the forest. We stopped after thinking we heard something behind us. Goldie was going on and on in the distance. "You hear that back there?" I asked.

"Was it a splash in the creek?" Cardy asked.

"I thought it was a scream myself but wasn't going to say anything," Delores said.

"I can't think straight for Goldie carrying on," I said,

"Lord, I don't want to think what's got her stirred up," Cardy said. We had been moving, following Blue until a fork in the path, where one way led up a hill. "I remember going downhill," Cardy said.

"Me, too," Delores said.

"Where's Ida?" I asked, turning back and peering into the darkness behind me. My aggravation at Goldie's noise was flickering and sputtering as those torches and our shadows.

"Ida!" Delores called suddenly. "Ida!" We each realized that we didn't know how long she's been missing. Blue bayed.

"When did we lose her?" Cardy asked, and it got quiet. I heard the fire sputter.

The harmonica song suddenly returned and drifted above us, in the distance, as if the player circled back around us and was returning in the direction from which we'd come.

"Shhh," I said to Delores when she opened her mouth to shout again. Blue started up again, "Shhh!"

"Maybe we were only following someone gone to fetch firewood or berries or water," Cardy said. "And now he's returning home." Blue whined and continued, as if we should follow him.

"Good," Delores said. "That means he'll lead us close enough back to our camp, we should be able to find it."

"What about Ida?" I asked. "We can't leave her!"

"Tie that piece of hide to the branch there," Delores said pointing. "We'll mark the way and come back to look for her after we make it back to camp first. We need to check on the camp by the sounds of it and then search for Ida."

We did what Delores said to do, but all we found was Goldie barking at us, and the camp was the way we left it. Ida wasn't there. I called out for her repeatedly, and no one answered, not even the harmonica player. I was racked with worry. The silence bothered me. I stalked back and forth along the route. I called. Back to camp for the third time in the night, I collapsed. I was sick that I would have to tell Benny she disappeared, that I lost her or she was taken.

At dawn, Ida hadn't returned. I told myself that it was unreasonable to imagine her being killed by a bear or a wolf. We mounted the horses and followed the same path. In a crevice of the hollow, I saw her body in the creek bed and gasped. I jumped off the horse and ran, red splash of dried blood, but I could see the faintest mist from her nose. She breathed. My hands on either side of her face, I called to her, "Ida."

Her eyelids flickered. "Sister," she said and smiled faintly. I could see the place where she had slipped and hit her head on the stone. She shivered in her wet dress.

Tentatively, we helped her onto the back of Gala with me. On the way, she said against my shoulder blades, "I dreamt of a golden woman. She was a Goddess in the forest with a fire under the rock. She poured waters over me from a bowl, and I knew that she had made the bowl for me. She had black hands, and she held them on my hips and my abdomen. Her head was as a buffalo. She told me the secrets of lovemaking so that I can have babies now. She said that there is no need for distress." Ida rested her forehead against my spine. At the camp, I dressed her wounds while Cardy and Delores made food and tea.

When we finished, Ida said, "Let's get to the buffalo arch. We need to go now."

~ ~ ~

The Devil Cried
Lyrics by Robin Ballard

I was wandering the woods coming up with a song
When I saw an old goat playing a tune too long.
You know the goat, branded and marked,
As if he's the reason the world's hate was sparked.
He had a fiddle, banjo, and guitar—
Played all to perfection.
And, I listened in a stupor of musical reflection
To all the tunes I loved, and sobbed
When I heard the truth of that story...
The Devil's stolen glory...
He said, "Oh, no, you've got it all wrong
That was never my song
Child of light and Morning Star—
They don't understand these scars.
No, the Devil hides out deep in the wild
I'm in the hollow, by the springhouse
And I never hurt nobody's child
I never started nothing, not this rouse
With the world, people, all that's crazy
Oh, no, I like the dirt and trees
And the snaky
Mazy way of the switchback trance.
I was never interested in all that rant
That people created
Because they hated

Themselves.
Oh no, it's not me, the Devil,
Nothing at all I did or said.
It's all in the inner dread
Of man, that's it, inside
A big missing part
Of his no-good heart.
No outside influence, no Devil,
No need for imagining demons to revel.
It's just people." He hung his head low.
He played the tune pitifully slow.
Hiding out, that's what he'll do for forever
Because that tortured story people won't sever
Their ties with. They use it to hide
All their own horror.
We sat by the creek's side
And I understood the sorrow
He had inside.
We made no barter or exchange
I played the same range
When we met as when I left
And a fiddle, banjo, guitar—all that he kept
I took nothin' but I listened to him cry
When we parted ways, singin' Goodbye...

Stinging Nettle

Medicine for disguise, or for disguise to be revealed

A trick happens upon
The mistaken certainty of smooth,
The comfort of taste to categorize.
An undulating slithering of soft breath
In the fruit, beneath the horse
Nettle, rising up, snake
Of a tree branch.

Thirteen | Dream Surprises

AFTER ATLANTA AND THEN THE OCEAN, I learned that many of the rewards of making music are in the journeys. The performances are surreal, sometimes almost out of body, at least in the beginning. However, each trip allowed me to get closer to people and revealed another layer about myself, my family's history and how it connected to me.

After our trip, we played our first session back at Love's Rest that Saturday night. It felt good to be playing at our home place. I was happy knowing what to expect about everything except Kevin. But, he was there. He sat at a picnic table outside under the trees. "He's waiting for you," Angie elbowed me.

"He's in our band, so he's waiting for *us*," I said.

Almost immediately after hearing about the trip, he told us that he'd like to try out a song he was writing. We all agreed because Love's Rest was our place for experimenting. The audience was always hospitable when we told them that we had something new. They even gave us the "so-so" sign when the song wasn't quite right yet.

Once he got the okay about the song from us, Kevin turned to me and asked to see the notebooks later. I hesitated. "I should have looked at them before," he said. So, I took that as an apology.

Being on stage with all of us again felt familiar and as if we had a newly charged energy, especially when Kevin played the harmonica and sang his new song. We listened and took it in as if he had written a lullaby. The audience loved it when he switched gears and led that song right into one that we wrote long ago together and that some of them already knew.

Aunt Melinda and Gordon came out to the show that afternoon, and I was shocked by the regulars who were becoming our fans.

"Hey Robin, we were at the Blue City. Great show!" a man shouted to us and pointed to his wife.

"Yeah?" I said. "You went to Chattanooga to see us, that's so cool. Thank you."

"Well, we was visiting there anyway," he chuckled, along with some of the audience, "and we saw y'all in the paper, that you'd be there, so we went. It was real good."

"I'm just gonna tell myself that you went down there to see our band. You're our new groupies, see, and we sure do appreciate it." The audience laughed. "By the way, for all you groupies, we've got another show scheduled next month in Knoxville at the Dueling Mantis Bar."

That evening, Kevin and I sat at the picnic tables under the hanging lights, while he read the section of Ma Zona's notebook that I had tried already to tell him about.

"I know this place," he said, pointing to the passage that she wrote about when they sewed the quilt. "It's the needle arch. Not far from the twin arches that I took you to." He tapped the page over and over. He whistled and his face turned red. "I don't know what to say," he said and placed his hand on top of mine. "She's definitely writing about where we went."

"Yeah, and the great door of stone, as she calls it."

"Yep, that was the first place. Sure seems like her description without all the sweeping." He laughed.

"You want to go back out there to the needle this time?" I asked.

"Sure," he said. "I'm off at the end of the week."

We drove out to the park again, and Kevin talked nonstop almost the whole way. He told me all about his dad, who was originally from Jamestown, raising horses and being a champion breeder, and even being famous in Tennessee Walking Horse circles. I knew about those from my family's history, though my people only seemed to dabble in it. They weren't as serious as what Kevin was telling me. Someone even shot one of his dad's horses, just so he wouldn't win.

"That's barbaric and cruel," I said.

"Yeah, my dad got out of the business after that," he said. "He sold everything and we moved."

"Might be more to that story," I said.

"Maybe," he agreed. "Being so closely connected to this place all those years, I learned a lot about it." He pulled alongside the road and parked at a trail marker.

"Slave Falls," I said, shuddering after reading the sign. "I can only imagine the horrors that happened there."

"Actually, it's not what you think," Kevin said.

I grunted in disbelief.

"It's not bad," he said. "Well, it's all bad when we're talking about people being slaves. But this area,

Slave Falls, is named that because runaway slaves went this way, through the wilderness, on their way to the North, and they hid in these rock formations and caves all around this area."

"Wow," I said. "You mean no one turned them in?"

"No, there were only farmers and hunters out here. Saltpeter miners."

"There wasn't a town at all?"

"One settlement. It was called No Business."

I gasped. "She mentioned that place," I said.

"Yeah, my dad told me and my sister that the people who lived there just kept to themselves. They were like wild people, but farmers, real country people. He said that nobody ever had any reason to fear the people of the wild because they worked so hard. They helped those who helped themselves, so a lot of people have always said that they helped the runaway slaves to escape through here." He shrugged. "I don't think anybody has ever proven it."

"It does seem unlikely in a place this far back in Tennessee," I said. "Confederate flags and all?"

"Well, they fought for the Union Army in the Civil War," he said. I must have looked shocked. "Yeah, the No Business people were poor and no one had slaves. They probably felt like slaves in some ways before they came out here to live because I imagine a bunch of them were sharecroppers and indentured servants, but I don't know for certain. Just going based on what I heard growing up." We walked down the path while Kevin told me what he knew about the place that it had been before it was a park.

"They even hid their sons from the Confederacy," he said. "There's some story about two brothers suffocating in a storage container when their mom tried to hide them from Confederate scouts. They were with the Union. This county even tried to secede from Tennessee because they didn't want to be part of the Confederacy."

"I never heard of that in my school classes," I said. "That's really surprising about the people here, how they felt and what they did about it. I'm impressed," I said. "And this is where your dad's family is from?"

"No, no," he said. "My dad is from Jamestown, not far away, and yeah, some of what I told you is true about the Jamestown area, too, but No Business was a town way out here. It doesn't exist anymore. My dad just always told us about the history. Like I told you before, my parents were obsessed with going to different memorials, Civil War battlefields, parks, and all that."

I enjoyed hearing more about Kevin and his family, but more than that, I liked writing with him. Our energy matched almost instantly when one of us started working on a song. I was bewildered that he knew how to complement my style, and it seemed so effortless for both of us to do for one another.

At the needle arch, I imagined Zona and her sisters sewing together, and I started a song about it for me and Angie. I messed around with the lyrics for about an hour. Kevin wandered down the trail away from the arch. When he returned, he flipped open his notebook and showed me "One Long Song" for us.

On the way home from the park, Kevin invited himself to tag along with me for the evening. I already had plans to eat a late dinner with Aunt Melinda and Gordon. Aunt Melinda and I made dinner together as much as possible, just the same as if Cora were still alive, the same as we always kept it.

"I love the new songs you've been writing," Gordon said over dinner at Aunt Melinda's house.

"Robin has these diaries," Kevin said, excitedly. "One of them is even like a spell book from her great-grandma. Those are the inspiration for the new songs."

"Whose diaries?" Aunt Melinda asked, as she took the pizzas out of the oven.

"We're always having pizza," I said, trying to change the subject without being obvious.

"It's the best pizza," Gordon said, placing napkins on the table. "That's why. And, when your great-great-aunt has saved this sourdough starter for thirty years, then you have to eat the pizza *always*."

"What do you mean saved the starter for thirty years?" Kevin asked.

"Cora," Gordon pointed to the stool where Cora sat, and I imagined her smiling now, "saved this sourdough starter and fed it for thirty years." He tried explaining the process to Kevin.

"It was probably more like sixty years knowing her," Aunt Melinda said, setting the pizzas on the table. "She was having trouble with the passage of time for years before she died. But who can blame her, she was ninety-nine years old."

"Ninety-nine," Kevin said and stared at her stool.

"I didn't realize that was her age," I said. "I thought she was a few years younger."

"Ninety-nine," Melinda said, gathering plates.

Gordon placed a glass of sweet tea in front of me and continued around the table.

"Whose diaries?" Aunt Melinda asked again, handing a plate to me. "Kevin mentioned diaries?"

"Ma Zona's," I said and realized that I couldn't avoid telling Aunt Melinda about them.

"My Mama?" I imagined Cora asked. I nodded.

"What?" Aunt Melinda and Gordon asked simultaneously.

"Miss Emy and I dug up a trunk of hers," I said. "Before I left for Atlanta, I decided to go out there to the medicine wheel and dig up that spot where the metal detector went off." I turned to Aunt Melinda, "You know, it was the day you drove out there and told me we'd be on Music City Mornings?"

"Really?" she asked. "I don't know what you're talking about."

"I was looking for that treasure from the Woods Runner," I said.

Cora nodded. "I remember that you were," she said.

"I sort of remember," Aunt Melinda said. "But go on. You said that you found Ma Zona's trunk?"

"Yeah, she buried it in the medicine wheel. I dug it up with Miss Emy, and Ma Zona put a bunch of journals in there, a recipe book, her tarot cards, jewelry, some other things in there."

"A spell book," Kevin said, joking.

"What do you mean a spell book?" Gordon asked, putting down a slice of pizza that was too hot to eat.

"Not a book of spells," I said. "It's about plants. I don't know how to describe it exactly."

"I want to see it," Aunt Melinda said. "You said her tarot cards were in there?"

"Yeah, they're cool."

"I remember those," Aunt Melinda said. "She would use them at the family meetings in the medicine wheel. I forgot how good she was at predicting the future. People would come to visit and ask her to do it."

"She was a fortune teller?" Gordon asked.

"No," Cora said.

"Oh, no," Aunt Melinda said. "She definitely was not that. She didn't like being called a fortune teller. She was a midwife and a healer, and that's what she considered herself. I vividly remember her explaining to me and my sister, Carolyn, that the cards were tools. The plants were also tools that she used, and she harnessed the medicine from the plants and the cards. Something like that."

"That's it," Cora said. "That's how she said it."

"She made us taste the different plants," Aunt Melinda said. "I liked the stinging nettle the best because I thought it would sting but it didn't. It was supposed to have something to do with disguises. I've always remembered her saying that. And she said something about blackberry protecting you." Aunt Melinda shrugged. "That's about all I remember." She glared at me across the table. "I can't believe you haven't told me."

"Or me," Cora said folding her arms across her chest.

"There've been so many things happening that I honestly just forgot," I said.

"I want to see it all," Aunt Melinda said. "Please."

"Yeah, of course. I left most of it at Miss Emy's."

"Now I aim to go, too," Cora declared.

~ ~ ~

The buffalo carved out the trace. We followed them. Ancestors hunted them from the sandstone, rising above the valleys. The arch was the perfect location to survey the land and the animals that allowed people to live from the land.

I kept sewing all the pieces into the blanket, adding the woods runner's strip of hide, but I don't know why they wanted us to sew it. We are doing what they asked us to do without asking many questions for why. Maybe if we had asked, I could have put the answers in here.

When we come across the bears, Ida whispered, "She told me in the dream." The mama stared right into my eyes. Those cubs were the cutest furry balls, playing and tumbling. That moment of suspended silence. Then, Blue started in a low growl. Goldie tipped that head down and pointed her tail straight out, and something ferociously afraid boiled down in her and wound out. I never heard her make a sound like that. Gala stamped backward. Coffee was already backing away with Ida, nothing to do but take him back. Delores rode the most steady boy, and I swear Glider wasn't afraid of nothing, and I half wondered if something was wrong with him in the head for that, but suddenly, as I was taking it all in, Delores aimed the gun at the mama bear. About that time, Cardy's Rufous was riled up and going back, too.

I shouted in a growling loud roar, while Blue and Goldie barked with me, not moving closer, just holding our ground, barking and growling. When I opened my eyes, the mama was gone with those cubs. Delores put her gun away. I swatted at her. I hugged Gala and petted her, "Will they come back?"

Ida nudged Coffee up and pushed Cardy on Rufous along at the same time. "Not likely," Ida said. "They're afraid." She looked at Delores. "I would be."

We turned back and stayed at the buffalo arch since we hadn't come more than a barnyard's distance from it, deciding that was better than anywhere else in the night. Next day, we'd get back to the village, stay a night or two, and head out. I was ready to get Gala back to stables and let her rest, that was for sure.

I dreamt that night of the high stepping horses, the Tennessee walking horses that Harold trained. First, I saw Harold and Cora riding with a family in a wagon pulled by mules and listening to a whippoorwill call. He halted the wagon and that made the baby cry. He hit Cora when the baby cried. Cora's face was blue and purple. Then, Harold went off and cared for famous stallions, far away, breeding some winners. I saw him riding and shoeing them, brushing them. He loved them horses. I saw him with Cora, their mules, and the baby eating blackberries in the dream.

That baby stopped eating those blackberries and just laughed at me. After that, I seen Cora put her baby on a buffalo mother, and she ran away from Harold. The buffalo stopped and breathed, and I could see her breath so I knew it was cold. Cora didn't shiver and I said, "Ain't you cold?" And, she turned from me. She said, "How could you do that to me?" I kept telling her that it was to protect the family.

That morning before day light, I woke up scared from the dream. I heard great horned owls and pulled back the blanket and looked out. The owl hooted and another responded. They got closer and closer together, but I couldn't see them. I listened and watched the shadows of the poplars offer space to the sunlight when it began to reach through the sky and the forest.

The whippoorwill sounded nearby, and I jumped up as if I'd been bitten. I knew what had to be done.

~ ~ ~

One Long Song
Lyrics by Robin Ballard and Kevin Crenshaw

Well, I was lost and wandered in
To a town that I had no business in.
I was downright tired and plumb wore out,
So I tried to find a barstool and a pint of stout,
But the place was shuttered and sealed up,
No one to be seen, no empty cups,
"Hello!" I hollered. "Howdy doo?"

"Yeah, whatdoye want? I see you!
And you ain't got no business here
Get on out and don't shed a tear.
Keep on going, don't look back,
You've got enough, you've got a sack
Looks to be full to the brim, all you need,
All you need
That will get you over to where you need
Where you need
To be
To be
'Cause you got no business coming up in here
No business on this land right here.
What brings you round these parts, hon?

'Cause we know things deeper than these hollers run."

I looked around and didn't find the source
Of the voice
that tried to warn me something so profound
As being deeper than I needed to be
In business that didn't belong to me,
But I couldn't see nothing
In the dark of that empty building
Where I went looking for a cold brew
Even on a hot day, I'd a taken a sip of stew.
I was thirsty and hungry from being out there
"I didn't come for nothing, I swear,"
I said to the dark and lonely place.
"I had to get out of the city, get out of the pace.
I took off and kept going,
Trying to escape the rat race,
Way out to this wild tangled place.
I've kept wandering and pondering.
What I'm doing here,
Kept going and risking it,
Fording creeks and crossing hollers,
Finding barns and watching swallows,
Jumping ditches and climbing banks,
Sitting on stones and giving thanks,
Shelling nuts and picking berries,
Swearing these woods are full of fairies,
I kept wandering and pondering
What I'm doing here,
Kept going and risking it,
Until I got to No Business here."

"Well, I can't tell you how to begin or end

But No Business is the place you're in
Now, and you might as well stay
It's been a long few days and a hard way.
I know what it's like out there
Especially when the weather turns from fair
And the trails are covered with icy snow
Just stay a while, it's so far to go.
I can see now you've some business to tend
Here in No Business where we don't have any men.
They've all gone away, far from the mines
In their place, grow the pines
Grow the pines
Here's a soothing drink
A soothing drink
A draught to sink
You into bliss and flip
Your sorrow with just one sip.
One sweet sip."

I was getting lured in
But my conscience chimed in
This voice is becoming a siren
An eerie omen,
"Thank you for the offer, ma'am, but I better go
I've got to cross a troublesome slick hollow
Between here and there
And I can see that I've got no business here
There's nothing out there to fear
So I've got no business being around here
No business being here."...

Yaupon

Medicine for laughing as the ancestors

We are brought together
Around a laughing tea
A black drink
For everyone.

Fourteen | That Luck

MARTIN INVITED THE banjo player to practice. I think it was so I would stop asking Martin to play it for some new songs. As he had told me from the moment I learned that he could play it, he wanted to stick with the bass.

I guess sometimes people are meant to become part of our lives and fill in the empty spaces. That emptiness often gets occupied right before a big change. Lucie had black, shaggy hair that fell in her eyes often. She smiled nervously, too much, and then realized it and stared down at her hands and her banjo, her shoes, the floor. It was awkward, but Kevin introduced himself. Once that happened, I felt like everything would flow smoothly between us. Maybe we all wondered if Kevin would be the person who was bothered the most by someone else joining the band, even if it was only temporary.

Almost as if she sensed it, Lucie said, slowly, "No need for worry, guys. I'm an exchange student. I'm here for only a couple semesters until I return home. I can play with you for little while. To fill in, as Martin and I agreed." She smiled and gestured to Martin.

"Where are you from?" I asked her. I liked her accent, her choppy way of speaking so it seemed like she was extra careful with the words she chose. She wore a soft green t-shirt and jeans, the rounded tips of her plain brown boots sticking out.

"Czech Republic," she said. "I'm here to study music business at the university," she said, and she gained momentum as she became more comfortable with us, so I chalked it up to nerves more than speaking English carefully.

"My name is Robin," I said. "I'm in school there, too."

"Oh, like the bird," she said. "Do you play the Rockin' Robin?" She laughed and began playing while singing. Everyone joined in, "Tweet, tweet a leet...cause we're really gonna rock tonight."

"Yeah," Kevin said. "We should add that one to our album, but we'll have to pay royalties on it." He laughed, and then surprising us all, he turned to Lucie and asked, "You available to record a few tracks on our new album?"

My eyes widened as I glanced at Angie, shocked that Kevin was offering to include someone in our album. Kevin was serious, and, of course, he began negotiations immediately. Lucie agreed to do it for a set fee and didn't want anything from future album sales. "You'll sign a statement saying that?" He asked. She nodded and laughed. "Today?" he followed up.

"Of course," she said.

That was a big deal for Kevin and he was bonded to her from that point. I doubted whether an album was going to happen, yet Kevin seemed confident where we weren't. He adjusted his ball cap. Martin looked on questioningly as Kevin seemed to be negotiating a deal that he thought was real and valid, not some imaginary, futuristic scenario that college students promise each other.

"Now that we've been on television, we need to record a real album, as close to full length as possible," Kevin said, shrugging his shoulders as if we should all know this.

Of course, we did all understand this already, but what we had was a demo with two songs that we pretty much made for ourselves. We couldn't very well sell that many demos to the public, unless we decided to put it on some online site that distributes music, and it wasn't that easy for a small band just beginning. We were hoping for a little break.

Aunt Melinda continued to shop us around, showing people the recording of the morning show and some of our live performances. Apparently, all of our work and fate came together like a group of pickers sharing the stage.

When we met at Love's Rest one Saturday, I told them the offer we finally got. "Aunt Melinda has been asking labels to consider signing us," I said. "She's a big fan of our music. She's got a lot of contacts, and when she sees people she knows in the industry, she tells them about us. Well, finally, this little record label said yes, pretty much. They watched a recording of the morning show and some of our live recordings that she has. They've got about four acts on the label, including one big star. That doesn't mean anything because I haven't heard of some of their other acts. We'll have to sell ourselves and see what happens, but at least, we'll actually have an album to sell at shows. Assuming we do alright when we meet them and all that."

"Your Aunt Melinda," Kevin said immediately, pointing to me and breaking into a grin.

"I know," I said. "She continued to persist and got us a record deal for one album, two days in the studio, and that's all they'll do for us. Maybe some merch," I said. "Very limited, but still a good deal."

Kevin covered his face, and I didn't know if he was laughing or crying.

"I'm lucky," Lucie said and then she played a little ditty on her banjo in celebration.

Angie made a strange hum-squeal with her eyes shut tightly.

Martin clapped his hands over and over, as he did when very excited about something. He hugged all of us, even Lucie. "Such great news," he said. "I knew it!" he said a moment later, hugging Angie again. "Time for some drinks to celebrate."

Kevin adjusted his ball cap.

"How did this happen?" Angie asked Kevin. "How can her aunt do this?" She tugged at the points of her maroon hair framing her face. She felt around the nape of her neck, as if her pixie hair might have changed after the new knowledge she had just received about our band. As if she were reading my mind, she said, "I feel so different, like I need to pinch myself to be sure I'm not in a dream."

"To our future success," Martin said, winking at her, and taking a sip from his flask.

"No pressure," Lucie said, taking the drink that Martin offered and passing it to Angie.

Martin clapped his hands nervously a few times, and Angie adjusted her hair, though it hadn't moved at all.

"When do we go into the studio?" Kevin asked. "We have a lot to practice."

"I agree, but don't know yet," I said. "We have to go in and meet them and sign the deal, basically. We'll have such a tiny amount of studio time that we've got to be focused so we don't squander it."

One of our fans showed up with a bundle of sage to smudge everyone at Love's Rest that night. She whirled it around the people outside. They were good-natured about it and stretched their arms out wide, turned around in a circle as she instructed them to, picked up their feet. Her sage wand went round. It was funny, and a first at a performance. "You know how heavy metal shows have dry ice?" the woman asked. "Well, this is the folk version of dry ice." She winked and laughed. "This keeps the bad vibes away." I thought of my relatives, felt as if they were sending me signals and good fortune.

"Well, get me again," a man said, giggling, while going back to the area under the trees where people stood waiting to be smudged by her.

~ ~ ~

Seal
Cardy
Craft the sentiments
Overflow the poetry
Waft the words
Pen the plans
Laughter
Effusive
Stamp each moment

Follow each lead
Express each place
Complete each crossroads
Speech
Elegant

I didn't want to let it go. Our Mamas told us that this was the time when the trace was ripe for pickin' our way through to the next stage. I believed it, or else my life didn't have much purpose beyond farming and birthing. Helping one's neighbors is always honorable, and yet there's yearnings in our hearts that need to complete some work on behalf of the Great Spirit.

That's why I insisted that we meet after a few years, to get on with it. Releasing the journey too early meant it might not hold. Everything had to be set right. I wrote the letters in the summer, and at first, none of them agreed. Ida was pregnant, again, and her children's nanny was raising Cain about another child. She's the only one of us to employ a nanny because she and Benny had the means. Death is a business, too. Ida had twins, first. Next was their three sons, almost three years in a row.

Delores was having too much fun lately with Dr. Landry. That's exactly what she had the audacity to write.

And, Cardy, she was the last to respond with this missive:
Dear—
I have a deadline.
Xx,

After I retorted to each, they agreed. Well, I'll be....
I expected more arguments and excuses, and they
proved me wrong. We would meet at the mushroom
rock when the leaves burned red and yellow in October.
Not only that, but Ida had a new tea that she wanted us
to try, and Delores would have time to travel.

Cardy again responded last with another scant
message:
Darling—
I have a surprise.
Xx,

I never told anyone about our journeys except
Hoot, and he never asked, "What for?" We only met five
times. It was barely a moment of my life each time, but
it was a reprieve for sisters to depend upon one another,
honor the ancestors, each other's imagination, and
Spirit's medicines.

The rain shattered the seed pods and broke them
open. Water slid along the leaves and slipped
underneath my cape and down into my boots. We left
my mules and the wagon in a barn, where we could also
sleep if needed, about ten miles from the mushroom
stone. The barn belonged to another of Hoot's cousins.
He wrote to him and asked if we could stay in the
autumn if we passed through on the way to
Chattanooga. He wrote back that his house burned
down, but we were welcome to use the barn to rest our
mules and get water out of the well. He was living about
twenty miles away with his sister til he got ready to
build another place out there. He was leasing the land
to hunters for a year or two, but nobody was coming til
the new year.

The barn was in good shape and looked as though nobody had bothered it. Them mules seemed a lot happier than me because they were staying dry.

Water poured and gushed the trails and fell off the ledges. We trudged and talked under the trees, knowing our supplies were mostly soaked. Delores assured us that she had ways. Ida did, too. They competed for knowing the most of ancestors' ways.

"Your letter," I said to Cardy as a way of asking about the surprise and if she still wished to tell it.

"When we make camp," she said, shouting above a long roll of thunder. The crack of lightning was close as we traversed the mountain's ridgeline. The cover of hemlock and pine, laurel and rhododendrons were welcome. I felt their living presence with a view magnificent for seeing the full valley and the passageways.

"This rain is good cover," Ida said. "Benny's people told me that this is a dangerous place for colored folks." She waved her hand at me. "Don't stare at me, Zona. I didn't tell why I was coming here, or that I was even going to be here. I made conversation about someone I know visiting here. This place kept giving me a feeling when I thought about it. I needed to check on it."

"I like the rain," Delores said nodding. "Mama said something similar about Signal. I think she did. She said to take care a few times. Didn't she?" Delores nodded again toward me.

"I don't know if it was here. I'm trying not to dwell on it," I said. "I want to complete the plan." I didn't want to acknowledge that this place and the conditions of our stay were shakier than our previous journeys. The rain aided in my feeling of foreboding.

As the rain slackened ahead, it whirled there in a little tunnel on the trace. The small yellow leaves from hackberries swirled up into it. Their trunks were knobby and dark, slicked with rain, but their leaves were bright yellow wedges whipping forward now. Cardy giggled and ran toward them, throwing open her arms and running ahead of us down the trail. It dipped ahead and she went on, laughing and sloshing through the mud and misty rain.

Ida smiled and leaned into her walking cane, taking off at a faster pace. Delores was charged by that and strode beside Ida, both of their faces set with determination to catch up with Cardy.

Feeling relieved, I sang a song to the rain that only we knew.

The rain that blew
The leaves
    Made you
Reach your arms out
    And float away.
            You laughed as you floated away
            Me, you, the rain and play
            We danced on a mountain
            In a perfect storm that day
            You laughed as you floated away
    The misty path called out
    To run this way
Open my arms wide
    And float away.
With the leaves
    We send our blessings
To float away.
HmmmHmmmHmmHmmmm. Float away.

We made up the songs until the rain dripped and the sun peeked through the forest in spots. Ripe persimmons dotted the ground, and I picked some up from among the fallen leaves and a few from the branches that I could reach.

"I've got ripe pawpaw," Ida said. I smiled, happy to share a custard fruit, as it has always been a favorite.

The mushroom stone acted as an umbrella for our camp. Cardy ran until she reached it before all of us. She had already unloaded a small log with kindling that she managed to keep somewhat dry underneath her clothes and blanket bundle.

The rain created a water curtain in places when it came on strong again. By then, we sat underneath the mushroom stone. We used hides to protect ourselves and our camp space, no matter where we ended up. Nowadays people don't need or use hides like that, but we needed them. They held up against rain and cold, especially, but heat and wind sometimes needed a layer between them and the skin, too. Mullein lined my shoes and clothes, creating a rain barrier, soft cushion, and giving extra warmth.

After we had some fire hot and dry enough, Delores made a laughing tea for us to share. We all took a drink from the same cup. Three times each unless it's not possible. There was enough water for each of us to have three times three. We laughed about this, but Cardy got the giggles and couldn't stop. She sounds like a little piglet when she giggles. I got so tickled about that I cried and fell over to the side. Delores said she almost peed herself, and I said that she probably did if she was saying almost, and that made Ida roar and cackle, which just started the whole thing over again.

The fire popped and that startled us into silence and laughing again, but not for long. The fire broke the spell. Delores said, "Cardy, this place seems to be about you."

"Oh," Cardy shooed her. "These places are about more than all of us and our future families. Even if it seems like one place had more of a message right then for one of us, they've all been beyond us. They're about more than the people we know and are connected to."

I agreed with that. It was the first reason, the only reason, that our Mamas gave us. I was glad that Cardy reminded us. "That's what our Mamas wanted us to do this for, Cardy. Something bigger than we can imagine."

"Your words were beautiful," Ida said to Cardy.

"That's what my surprise was about," she said.

"What surprise?" Delores asked looking at me.

"I wrote to Zona that I had a surprise." They looked at me inquisitively.

I said, "I don't know the surprise. She didn't tell me what it is, just that she has one."

"Well, what is it?" Ida asked, giving me a wink and turning to Cardy.

"I'm an author. I'm using a man's name, a pen name, and I get paid." She squealed and threw her hands up. "Can you believe it?"

We sat there dumbstruck. "There's more," she smiled. "I have a son, Alex. I'm married, but Alex wasn't his. I did bleed at the arch, but I don't know if it didn't work or if when I saw the hunter again, well, you know, surprise."

"You put something in this tea?" I asked Ida. She glared at me, as if insulted by my question. I gestured to

Cardy, wondering if her story came from what she'd been drinking. Ida shrugged.

"You don't believe me, do you?" Cardy asked us.

"How?" Delores asked. "How did you do that? Have the hunter's baby and start writing books as a man?"

"I don't write books. I write stories in a column, and I don't know, something came over me. I wrote in to an editor, sent him my story, and said I was a man. He mailed me a check, and I waited to tell him the truth. It was a riot when he found out I was a woman, to say the least. And, then we married."

"The editor's your husband?" Ida asked.

Cardy nodded. "He's older. Twenty years. Twenty-nine to be exact," she laughed and blushed, as if she were the one robbing the cradle. "A.J. never found a wife before. I guess girls thought he was a square even when he was a boy. I think he's funny, and he makes me and Alex laugh a lot."

"Did you maybe know him before you wrote the letter and something came over you?" Ida asked, teasing her.

Cardy narrowed her eyes and smiled in her jaw line. "Yeah, I knew him a little. Even though Alex isn't his, he wanted a son and treats him as if he is. They're off on their own adventure right now. Philadelphia," she said proudly. "A.J. has a nephew there."

"What are your stories about?" Delores asked.

Cardy poked at the fire. "Hunters, quests, wild animals, untamed lands, and adventures. Sometimes folks mail a letter and request a certain type of story. I've obliged a couple of times," she said.

The mushroom stone was a signal, as if entering a child's land of imagination and giggling. We played games with stones and sticks, pulled the cards and closed our eyes into the shimmering pools of the future, watched the full moon behind the clouds as they ran swiftly across the sky, pulling the smokestacks of trains and cities in the distance. The eye of the moon watched over us. The branches tapped and squeaked out tunes while we sang, holding hands, falling time and again over something funny someone said, and sharing our soggy supplies.

The next morning, we knew it was complete as the hawk cried out and circled the valley. The sun lit up the leaves, this time illuminating the red and orange tips. Our walk was quieter on the way back. The restlessness we had when we arrived was gone with the rain.

By noon, we reached the barn and the mules looked content, happy to see us, and we felt the same. I was completely relieved then. Delores said, "It feels like this trip passed too quickly."

"Yeah, this was quick," Cardy said. We hitched the wagon up and took off.

"No bad luck on this part of the journey happened," Delores declared to Ida.

"It's not over yet," Ida said. "You shouldn't make declarations until the quest is complete."

I was taking everyone as far as Nashville to Cardy's home. And since Delores planned to catch a train out of there to Louisiana, we stayed with Cardy for the night, boarding the mules. We escorted Delores to the station the next morning, and she was ready with her hat, gloves, and fan.

Ida and I continued to the Kessee place north of Nashville, where it was a moment of bliss to rest somewhere that was like home in my past, reminding me of Mama. Ida and Benny had a comforting presence, even with all the kids. Nobody arguing or messing around. The children helping each other. Maybe it's the consideration of death so often, as your way of life, as it was for Ida and Benny, that it makes you know what's important.

When I finally got back to my house, a telegram was waiting for me from Dr. Joseph Victor Landry, my brother-in-law. Somewhere between Memphis and New Orleans, Delores fell and struck her head, and was apparently robbed either before or after. No one saw a thing, they said, until after she was bleeding and unconscious. My sister was in the hospital in New Orleans, and she was asking for me to come there.

Mayapple

Medicine for shelter

Hide under the umbrella leaf canopy,
You, green forest floor
Wild lemon fruits.
Your fragrance releases
Tart sauce. Raccoon berries,
We shelter and save you
For late summer tastes,
For autumn jelly that glistens.

Fifteen | Nary a One

I SAW MORE. I was reading two of Ma Zona's books at the same time—what Kevin called *the spell book*, with the individual plants, descriptions, and recipes, and the book of places that she journeyed to with Delores, Ida, and Cardy.

I was still reeling about her confession—that she changed Cora and Harold's lives all because of a dream—unbelievable. Yet, that's exactly what she seemed to admit in her writing about the buffalo arch.

Equally shocking in my own life, I saw that those plant descriptions I read in Ma Zona's spell book were living dreams. I'd stop turning the pages on a plant, like Mayapple, and then soon after, I was reminded that it was some part of my life or it suddenly showed up where it had never belonged.

Miss Emy prepared a family meal for Thanksgiving and asked me, Aunt Melinda, and my dad to be there. Usually, he stayed at the shelter and served food, but this time, he agreed, as long as Aunt Melinda would give him a ride. His contribution to the dinner was, none other than, Mayapple jelly.

When I asked him about making it, he said, "Once a forager, always a forager."

The same happened for other plants, and I tried to go back through the book from when I first opened it. They seemed to connect to some meaning in my life. I flipped through the other books. Another was more plants and recipes, but without the extra incantations.

"Without the spells," Aunt Melinda said, raising her eyebrows. While Miss Emy and my dad talked and took time to catch up, Aunt Melinda and I went up to my old bedroom, where I had spread the contents of the trunk on my bed.

"Well, they're more like medicine spells," I said.

"Before I forget, I've got this DNA test for both of us to do," Aunt Melinda said. She handed me the swab for my mouth. "I wish that I had done this for Aunt Cora before she passed," Aunt Melinda said. "She really wanted that."

"She would be happy that we're doing it," I said. "With the results of this and the notebooks, we're going to know a lot more than we did." We sealed the swabs in their envelopes.

"Oh, you have her tarot cards here, too?" Aunt Melinda asked, looking around.

I pointed to the bundle, wrapped in a scarf. "This is everything that was in the trunk."

"That's the trunk?" she asked, looking amused at the small rusted metal container beside my closet door, exactly where Miss Emy had left it after hefting it up the stairs that night.

"The one," I said.

Aunt Melinda shook her head side-to-side and reached for the bundle of cards. She stopped. "Have you looked at them?" she asked.

"Yeah," I said. "They're pretty."

"I can't believe this," she said, untying the scarf. Her hands trembled. She smiled and a tear slid down her cheek. Then, another. "Miss Emy," she shook her head. "She was so angry." She wiped the tears away.

"She seems okay now," I said. "She was afraid back then." I knew that she was talking about the time Miss Emy forbade her and Carolyn from using the cards, and then Aunt Melinda and Carolyn moved their stuff into Ma Zona's house. Miss Emy was furious, but when she told me the story, I knew that she was more afraid of what she didn't know.

Aunt Melinda nodded. "I think so, too." She closed her eyes and shuffled the cards. She paused, then took my hands and placed them on the cards. Her hands rested on top of mine, and her eyes were closed.

She released my hands, opened her eyes, and turned over the top card. It showed people playing music and singing in front of a garden, but the sky was dark and carried a full moon.

"I think that's about you," she said.

"Dessert!" Miss Emy shouted up the stairs.

Aunt Melinda looked annoyed. "You," she tapped the card. I shrugged.

"Dessert's ready," my dad called to us.

Aunt Melinda gave me a worried look. "You okay?" she asked, referring to my dad.

"Yeah," I smiled. "He's sober and this has been good."

"I always worry about him coming back here," she said. "I think it brings back a lot of memories that make him feel bad, and I hate that. I think he struggles more after he comes back here."

"I never considered that before," I said. She placed the cards back on the bed and motioned for me to follow her.

Downstairs, Dad and Miss Emy sat in front of cups of coffee and dessert plates with slices of cake. They talked about the weather predictions and plants.

"I saw the signs," Miss Emy was saying. "Spoons in the persimmons. Hornet nests on the ground. Solid black caterpillars sparkling like snow."

"Yeah," Dad agreed. "Spoons in all the persimmons I had, too. Gonna be a bad winter." They referred to the weather signs—when a ripe persimmon is split in half and it looks as if there's a shovel or scoop inside of it, that means there will be a lot of snow.

Dad looked up and into my eyes when I sat down. He reached out his hand across the table and held mine. "I'm sorry for all the times I hurt you, Robin," he said. I didn't expect that and pulled my hand away, more from the shock than anything else. His eyes shone from the tears that filled them, but he didn't cry. "You're the best thing ever happened to any of us. I mean it."

~ ~ ~

I wouldn't stay in Louisiana once Delores was released from the hospital. Too many spirits. At the hospital, I made myself helpful to the nurses and they let me stay with her. She was in the corner of a big room, and they slid a little half cot back and forth from under her bed for me to sleep on.

My sister only had Dr. Landry, and as a surgeon, he was in New York and Philadelphia more than he was in New Orleans. He was skilled in repairing hernias and other delicate tasks. Delores didn't need one of those operations.

I had never asked, and I thought that Dr. Landry couldn't father children, but Delores told me different during that time we spent together. She said they didn't want to be parents. They enjoyed being out on the town, dancing and listening to jazz, even went to the Pythian Temple regularly, and delighted in one another's company too frequently to dote on children. "I don't ever want to nurse anyone," Delores said. As Dr. Landry returned to New York while she was in the hospital, Delores asked to come home to Granville with me for awhile.

Ida and Cardy wrote letters, asking to help with Delores. Both of them visited. Taking care of Delores, we questioned whether to go on to the other places and complete the protections.

Finally, we decided to make the trip to the falls. We chose a year of spring rain, so the creeks created some good falls all the way. Before we got there, we had to go from town in Spencer and then take a trace to the falls, a whole set of waterfalls during a good rainy season and even a flooding when it set to storming some years. From there, we'd either go back to Spencer, depending on the encounters along the way, or go on to Lee, where we could catch the train. This time, we didn't have any family out there, but I figured Granville is close enough.

We had left the station and walked down an old rutted farm road. Cardy said, "What do you know about this community? You think I could pull off living here?"

"Why?" Delores asked. "You've got A.J. and Alex."

"You think they need a writer here?" Cardy asked.

"You beat all I ever heard tell of," Ida said.

"Yeah," I said. "Most of these folks can't read or write. I'd say they need a school teacher."

"I've never met nary a one as you, Cardy Headman. Nary a one," Ida said, stopping in front of a thicket blocking the way.

"You and A.J. making each other jealous?" Delores asked and used her walking stick to push through the thicket and hold it back.

"He flirts," Cardy said. "I don't."

"You don't need to," Ida said.

We picked our way out the road and tried to listen and stay off it, just so folks didn't ask who we were and what we were doing. It didn't take long to get out to the wilderness and it split at a crossroads and dipping down into a hollow, the creek become so loud that we couldn't hear the wagon approaching. We hid. As soon as they were gone, Ida said, "I didn't think this was a good idea, remember?"

Sure, enough, then another wagon came along with a whole family. They were pleasant enough and one waved at us through the woods. Ida placed her back flat against a tree. Cardy leaned into the trunk against her side, as if she might casually be resting in the forest. Delores kept walking, not bothering to look. She thrust her walking stick forward, her wavy black hair frizzed around her head, sweat dripped from her nose and circled her neck. She ploughed ahead, snapping sticks. The father tipped his hat. And, another passed right after, and we didn't have time to even try to get into the trees. When a fourth wagon passed by, Delores said,

"Excuse me, gentlemen, there sure have been a bunch of passersby today. It looks to be a busy one." Two older gentlemen sat on the bench.

"Yes, Ma'am," the driver said, signaling for the mules to slow down. *"I reckon they're expecting a big crowd for the picnic."*

"I reckon they are," I said.

"How you think it got to be so big?" Delores asked, fishing for information, but they didn't seem to notice.

"Reckon everybody's done told somebody," the same man said.

"Printed it in yesterday's tattler," the other man said. *"Skipping Crow's Fantastical Show."* I didn't know what that meant and shrugged when Delores looked at me quizzically.

"I heard it at church," Cardy piped up. Delores glared at her.

"Which one was it?" the first man asked her, but she tripped on a rock about that time.

"I saw it in the newspaper, too," Delores said.

"Cain't hardly call it a newspaper," the driver said. The other man held up one page.

"Should be getting there soon," I said, as luckily a motorcar motored past us waving, with a long line of different vehicles behind it, bicycles and wagons, buggies, and horses.

"Wow," Cardy said. *"Can you believe a motorcar? Must be some important picnic."*

The men were gone and we continued the walk. At the next fork, we arrived at a long road where the wagons and horses that passed us were now resting. We could see a large lawn down the hill with blankets spread across the grass, children running and playing chase, and on a lawn to the right, we could just make out a baseball game and hear the crack of a bat, claps from the audience, more shouts and laughter as families and friends arrived.

"The food smells so good," Cardy said.

"Isn't there some rule about not stopping to eat with strangers when you're on a quest?" I asked. "I think there is."

"Rules?" Ida scoffed. "Music sounds good, too."

"Yeah," Cardy said.

"Zona?" Delores asked, nudging me toward the crowd. I patted the map in my pocket, silently promising that we would get right back on track after stopping briefly at this picnic.

"You just enjoy showing off your fancy clothes and shoes," I said to Ida.

"I do," she smiled.

"You don't have a do-rag anywhere in your home," I said. She laughed, knowing it was true.

As we followed the crowd toward the music, we noticed a gathering around a small tent with a banner on top, "Skipping Crow's Fantastical Show." It cost a nickel each. Peeking inside, we could see that a band was warming up on a small stage. The show was set to start in an hour.

"I haven't seen a traveling show since I was real little," Ida elbowed me and winked.

We sat for the dinner on the ground, after getting in the line and fixing plates of peas, cucumbers, beans, and barbeque, and everything you'd expect. I looked around for us a place to eat away from the crowd. I saw an old Granny by herself, and we sat with her.

"Mind if we join you?" I asked. She reminded me of my Mama in the way her face set, chiseled as stone, and her white hair flowed down her neck.

She nodded. "Young'uns all out there somewhere. Kids grown, grandkids, some of them is growed up, too, even some great-grandkids. I'm alright over here by myself, I told them." She smirked and shrugged to me. "You knowed I wished one of them would've sat with me though." I nodded. She squinted and her black eyes stared into mine, then she watched Delores and Cardy. "That your daughter?" she asked Cardy.

"Who?" Cardy asked, beside herself.

"She's your daughter," the Granny said, pointing to Delores. Cardy looked like someone had socked her, while Delores beamed like a young girl with candy. Ida had to look the other way to keep from laughing aloud.

Turned out, the Granny was the mother of the man who owned the farm where they were having the picnic. The family come round to check on her before the show was about to start, and she told them that now she was aiming to sit with us during it. That tickled Delores and Ida, but they were good about it and didn't let on.

When we got to the tent, one of the men collecting money stopped Ida, put his hand right on her chest, said, "You gotta wait in the back, ya hear?" He pointed to a couple of seats over to the side. I stood in line behind her, so he glared at me as if I might be next or maybe he hadn't decided yet.

"That nickel looks the same as those others," Ida said, retrieving her money from his palm and stepping away from him to get his other hand off of her.

We all turned to leave, for if Ida wasn't allowed in, then we weren't going either.

"Come on," the Granny said, motioning us forward despite the man's insistence. He looked back and forth between Ida and me and the Granny. Delores and Cardy waited, and people began to stare and inquire about the ruckus that we seemed to be starting. Whispers reached me.

"Mama!" we heard the man shout from the front of the tent. "Now, you're holding up the line! Your seat is up here." He was the man who owned the farm, her son, and the whole family was already at the front of the tent. The Granny trained her eye on him and wouldn't budge, so he made his way to retrieve her.

"I need seats for my friends, too," she said, when he reached her. "Or, I'm not sitting up there. And, I need you to pay this man, so he'll quit bothering us." Ida returned her nickel to the man's palm, even though the Granny's son gave him a quarter, paying for all of us again.

"Put some more seats up there for Mama!" the son shouted up to the family in the front. They shuffled around.

The son waved us forward. "Now, it's all fine, Mama. Just y'all, come on, will you?" He wiped the sweat from his brow with a handkerchief. The Granny took hold of Ida's arm and led us to seats near the front row.

In the tent, it was getting quiet again and dark where they draped the sides down. A spotlight shined up on the black wooden stage and the crowd became silent. A fiddler played as if someone was walking down a dark, lonely place at night. This crow walked out the length of stage, pensive, as if it were a man with his hands behind his back, reflecting. That fiddler then told *a whole story while the crow acted it out, dancing and skipping, that's where they got the name, and then another crow joined him, a girl. They were in love. It made us all real somber and sad when they finished the story, the girl crow dying in the skipping crow's arms.*

The crow hopped around carrying a hat and collecting a lot of coins. Ida whispered, "I believe they've got a flock." Looking around, I noticed other crows among the crowd.

"The Fantastical Show shall now begin!" a voice suddenly bellowed from the stage. I turned back and saw a woman dressed in shimmering gold, descending from the top of the tent above the stage. She sat on a big silver hoop, as an acrobat, and the bottoms of her feet were folded into the hem of the dress. Sleeves covered her arms. When she moved slowly, the gold scattered light and colors. Her hands contained patterns and designs, a tapestry, in black ink. She wore a little crown on her head, and a gold fan was attached to it, pointing downward and opened, concealing her face. Tiny designs were cut into the fan, allowing in speckles of light, but we couldn't see her face.

She slid off the hoop and walked the stage, back and forth, while music played and light danced. The silver hoop lifted and lowered again, and black crows perched on it. The crows flew in patterns across and up, swirling, following the movements of her hands. If her fingers turned, the birds spiraled. If her hands swept up, the birds went to the top of the tent. If her hands flickered down, the crows flapped up and down and up and down beside her. Finally, her hands imitated mouths speaking, the music stopped, and those crows said, "Watch." The audience gasped.

"*Watch!*" *the voice called that had introduced the show earlier. I did not see the source of the voice, but there were deep shadows around the stage.*

The crows said, "Watch," again when the golden woman made a motion with her hands. The music changed, and a poof of smoke startled us. The woman disappeared from the stage in an instant. A golden crow stood in her place on the stage. The other crows were gone. The audience applauded, but the music began again. When that golden crow raised her left foot, a regular crow appeared on the left side of the stage. She did the same with the other side. She used her wings to make motions that those black crows had done when the golden woman was there. I'll tell you what, that was some show to captivate every single one of us in the tent.

After it was over, they announced that folks could pay a quarter and see the woman's face behind the fan. There was a long line. Only Cardy wanted to see her face, so we didn't wait.

"*Most beautiful I ever seen,*" *someone said behind us, as the crowd dispersed.*

We didn't even have words when we left the picnic. Silently and hurriedly, we all walked about a half a mile until finding the trail that would take us to Cane Creek.

"*You think those were sound effects?*" *Cardy asked.*

"*Believable,*" *Delores said. Ida grunted. We continued down a narrower path, not much of a road at all. We had to pick our way through the rhododendrons and laurel, walking the creek bed at the bottom.*

"*That Granny thought I was your Mama,*" *Cardy said disgusted.*

"You do look old and then young," Delores said. "You always have, as if you switch back and forth somehow."

"That Granny was about near a hundred," Ida said.

We took our time crossing the creeks, and we could tell by the mayapples that covered the path that it wasn't the well traveled route, if there was one at all to this place. I took out the map. I carried it since the time I was courting, even sewed it into the pocket of a field dress for a while before I married. I made a fresh copy recently and left it in the cave, where Nenny showed me to hide what's important. When I unfolded it, the sunset made it look golden.

"What do you think the woman looked like?" Cardy asked dreamily.

"She looked as any other pretty woman," I said. "They used that fan to make more money because it makes folks think she's prettier than usual."

I studied the map and saw the spot where they marked the moonbow. Mama, or someone in the past, placed a rainbow through the moon. It was drawn over a waterfall.

We waited for the moon to rise, large and full. It was near midnight when it reached up and cast colors above the creek where the water spills over the edge. Quietly, we held hands underneath the moonbow. A crow called out and landed in a hemlock near us. We squeezed one another's hands. Another crow flew in and landed above the first. When it called, the sound was eerily similar to the word, "Watch."

~ ~ ~

Nary a One
Lyrics by Robin Ballard and Kevin Crenshaw

I said, "You must've been in love plenty of times,
Must've given the girls all those rhymes.

But you said, "There's nary a one as you.
I didn't tell 'em my heart's confession
I didn't show one of 'em my devotion.
Nary a one. No, not nary a one."

Well, I said, "You must've been to Lover's Leap,
Must've been holdin' hands in your sleep,
Not pining for beauties,
Not making up rhymes for imaginary cuties.
You must've been,
Someone like you must've been."

"No, not me, not nary a one
Of those things is true, you see,
Not nary a one.
Not nary a one is true for me.
There's no one like you
In my mind through the day
Nary a one as you.
There's no girl who can stay in my heart like you.
No, nary a one as you.
Nary a one as you..."

Honeysuckle

Medicine for revelry

Twirl and twine
And drift in thine
Own joyful glory.
A countryside blooming
To make cheap wine. To sing
In drunkenness under muddy
Riverside moonlight with heavy
Cricket songs. The green tips
Of the flower stamens glow as if fireflies
Dripped their iridescent flicker—tiny dips
Of nectar on each tongue. To recall
When we drink in autumn
The original concentration for pleasure.
To remember to dance among the honeysuckle,
Honeysuckle vines.

Sixteen | Purification Song

OUR BAND WAS going forward, looking into the future with enough space for all of us to make music the ways we needed to. We recorded a full length album, two days in a recording studio with an engineer, a pretty popular one, and we thought that would be our big break. It took months to prepare, but such a short time to create the whole album, the versions of the songs that people buy.

I thought everyone would be so grateful to record an album that working it out would be easy. Oh, no, we argued going into the studio about which songs to record and whether to record any covers. Back and forth with the label and each other, it took a week to agree, and we never really did. I don't know how some of the compromises managed to work out the way that they did. I tried to stand firm on the original songs, not doing the same old covers for our first album.

Nothing much changed when the album came out except that we were really excited and kept expecting to be discovered even more, again, by more people. I was exhausted by the need to be discovered around every corner.

I felt foolish later, and very naïve, but I believed in our potential for fame. I thought the magic combination was the full length album and the missing part, the banjo. It wasn't fame and lots of money that I thought about, though that would have been appreciated, but more about being liked by people, our music being remembered and sung by a crowd at a performance.

Getting small gigs had been pretty easy in Nashville after our appearance on Music City Mornings and recording the full length album. Lucie was along for the ride, so we could count on a banjo player for a little while longer, until the next summer, when she would return home to Czech Republic. We went to neighboring middle Tennessee towns and played in stores, everything from privately owned art galleries to record shops, and of course, bars.

I dreamt of playing at the Ryman and on the Opry stage. All through my childhood, I would have vivid dreams at night when I was under the heat of the lights and couldn't see the people in the crowd through the brightness and aura. A few of the dreams were bad, and I dropped my guitar onto the stage and once it fell right off into the crowd in the front row. Maybe that's one of the reasons why I always wanted that lucky strap. I never wanted to wake up from those dreams, even if the guitar fell or I tripped again on the stage, and in one dream I bloodied my nose, and when I did rouse from those deep slumbers, I shut my eyes again and tried to pick up where the dream left off.

I was floating on the stage, as if I had entered Heaven, a place filled with bright warmth that caused me to sweat in purification and song, where I sang to no time and no end, and the resonance of my soul escaped into the space without effort and came back to me as an echo filling me with a beauty that bloomed more melody and harmonized with the mystery of sweet existence.

That wasn't what my real songs were like. I didn't write those sweet little Gospel numbers with Heavenly angel choirs. I was trying to get closer to the real life that I saw and experienced.

~ ~ ~

The cave, the place where the meteorite struck in prehistoric times, dipped under the ledge, bowed, softened over time by many bellies, many seekers. Nenny led me to the rock shelf. She showed me the ancient drawings and burnings.

The winter challenged our travels. Yet, we went out in the cold early that year on account of Ida having so many babies. That February it had warmed and even set us in the mind of spring. We chatted pleasantly, never suspecting the changes.

On the first night we were there, the crows came in across the fields and through the forest. We watched them call in near a hundred and Delores said, "There's ice coming."

"Ice!" I exclaimed. "Why do you think that?"

"It's the sky, and the way the dark birds gather. They plan to huddle," Delores said.

The next morning, the red-winged blackbirds flocked to the edges and layered the cedar tree branches. We heard the ice approaching as if the trees clinked together little glasses. That tinkling sound so sweet and inviting but the cold penetrates as it encases.

Ida said that the cave needed to be shrouded, the carvings and drawings, the visions—"Some passages are between places that don't need to be connected anymore," she said. "Then, we can all move on and create anew. I see the snakes and horned ones in my dreams, and I am not afraid of them. They are both tiny and large. I understand this to be true. Guides. In the dream world, I see the invisible. Maybe this helps to comprehend its existence. You can be trained even if some of us are born with the sight for listening."

She wanted to protect the cave's medicine and change the route. We visited the breach into the earth, but we didn't know the entire route. It's warm inside the cave in the winter. Our fires light the walls, and all those ancestors.

"I worry about what I hear from the future," Ida said. The cave dripped. "Some invisibles are ghosts. Some aren't. Some bacteria. Some parasites. All visible depending on how you look, smell, listen. We are the dust we carry, but in the future, people disguise it."

"I never did see nobody what people said they look like," Cardy said. "I see what they sound like, what they feel like. That energy lives inside them. I see that no matter what they present on the outside."

Ida brought the honeysuckle wine, saved from summer flowers, and passed it around to us. We sipped and remembered, got warm and trembled, laughed and danced, sang as if in a trance underground, deep under the ground.

Our voices and our songs in the cave buried into the walls. Sound reached up to the ceilings and stuck there. We stayed at a farm nearby, in an old cabin by the creek. The ice kept us there for near a week.

"Worried about Cora?" Ida asked all of a sudden one day.

"What to do?" I shook my head.

"Harold Flynn never stopped coming around," she said. "You know he's been working for Hoot."

I already knew that he visited Cora for nigh fifteen years, on account of him delivering shine and whiskey. I never could understand why it worked that they didn't conceive a child for so long and then they did. I was mad as a hornet, though I didn't know what made it so.

"Could be someone else's," Ida said. "But don't seem likely."

"Why now? What went wrong?"

"His planting went right this time," she said.

When the warmth finally arrived, I was up earlier than anyone else. The red-tail hawk pierced the dawn with a shriek and continued to call. I made tea, replenished the fire, and waited. I knew it was all ending for our journey. Ida had too many babies, and I did, too. Dr. Landry was staying at home, and Louisiana was becoming farther away for Delores. And, Cardy wanted to settle down and stop the jealous games she played with A.J.. We still had one place's medicine to protect. Yet, the settling was starting.

It's the way the weeping willow shimmered in the sunlight that morning. The frost and ice melted slowly with the early morning's progression. I was still waiting for the words to come. I stood, mesmerized, as the branches swayed in the wind, scattering light. I was tempted to take off outside walking and forget my companions. My gaze drifted to the particles of moisture floating in the air, and the minutes mounted to nothing. A line of ice and frost receded, backing up across the field line, perfectly straight as the sun rose over the treetops. The frozen line slunk back, sun slid *forward. Melting, dissolving, and slipping down each brown stalk from last summer's efforts. The soil was wet and waiting as the sun combed forward, arriving overhead each day until warmth helps seeds to break forth again.*

~ ~ ~

This couldn't be right. Cora told me that she never saw Harold again. I shook the book as if it were a person. I wanted more answers about Cora. I took the journals to Aunt Melinda and told her everything that I knew. She narrowed her eyes at me. "I feel like ringing your neck for keeping this from me," she said. "I would've liked to have known that she was my grandmother." She stood up and put on the kettle to distract herself from being angry with me.

"I'm sorry," I said. "It was her secret to tell."

"I think it's selfish of you," she said. "She was old."

"Old or not, it was her story, not mine."

She sighed heavily, letting it go. "I'm making rose tea. You want some?" she asked.

"Please," I said.

After she made tea, she set to work on helping me figure it out. "Seems like Aunt Cora didn't tell you the whole truth," Aunt Melinda said, tapping her fingernail on the book. "Grandma. That seems crazy. Anyway, she probably didn't know how to tell the truth by then. She lied about it for so long."

"Yeah, but, wow," I said, sipping my tea. "She told me that she was my great-grandmother, so she could have just said that they saw each other for fifteen years. Why make it seem as if it was all in one summer?"

"Maybe she didn't mean it that way," Aunt Melinda said. "She was getting her timing all confused for a few years, at least. Who knows how mixed up it got in her mind? Maybe she thought she told you it correctly." Aunt Melinda shrugged. "The point is that she was my grandma, your great-grandma, and that's amazing. She told. That is almost unheard of."

She lifted her cup and closed her eyes, inhaling the fragrance of the rose tea.

I decided that I wasn't going to stop myself from saying what is, in life and in song. I saw how much Cora limited her mind with how she changed the truth to survive. That made me practice opening my mind more when drafting songs, even if I knew that I wouldn't always finish or use them.

Unheard Of Love
Lyrics by Robin Ballard

I listened to her stories
By her side
When she shared her memories
She revealed it all
An unheard of love
For years, she lived ashamed.
She was lonely and tired
When she broke down
And told me about her
Unheard of love...

~ ~ ~

Recovery
Lyrics by Robin Ballard

She shivered that morning
When the sun rose up warning
Lonely days lay ahead
More sleeping alone in her bed
War ain't got no heart
To reunite those in the fight

They say the sun shines red
When a warning is up ahead
Mornin' comes up rust
And the day'll be a bust

She got the message when the signs were up
Welcome Home
And the presents.
They even had a new pup.
She felt sick when
The men in uniform
Were at the door.
Her son said, "Don't play a trick.
We're picking Daddy up at four."
She pleaded and she explained
To their son that he wasn't ever
Coming back again.

She looks for signs of good luck
But instead she was stuck
With the bad news of those who lose.

She wanted four-leaf clovers and lucky hats

She wanted rainbows,
The nine lives of cats.
She wanted a discovery,
treasure troves,
a recovery,
But she'd take a second chance,
To have a glance,
a dance,
Any moment to be entranced
With him one more time
One more moment in time...

~ ~ ~

The Mirror Stars and Scars
Lyrics by Robin Ballard

She frowned in the mirror
At her reflection
Where her mother could see her.
Mama looked over her shoulder
Smiled into her eyes and told her,
"Say you'll take care
Swear
To love your body first
Give yourself joy and trust
Say you'll love you
Say you'll take care
Swear
To love your body first
Give yourself joy and trust
Because in the mirror stars
You.

The mirror stars
You.

Just because he said it one time
It would become a thing
Their relationship was based upon
Even if he didn't mean
She wasn't pretty as a nonblonde.
So, she altered herself
Bleached her hair
Twenty times a year.
She changed what she could
Nip, tuck, and strip away
Make it look the way he said it should
Tip, pluck, and selfie today.
She wore fake eyelashes longer than Pinocchio's nose.
She swore those zirconium earrings were diamonds
from Granny Rose.
Fake fingernails, tattooed eyeliner
She made appointments
Modern anointments
But in all these answers
There was none unkinder
To her image in the mirror
Than the one to fear her.
Those eyes looking back
Were the first to attack.

She tried every meditation class.
Learned the spiritual answers, a test to pass,
She attended cross fit
And watched that fitbit.
Every step she took

Turned into another hook
Into her flesh, her skin, her scars,
She tried to hide the cuts, the wars
She inflicted on her body
Her no body
No body

The sleeves, they covered her arms
Concealing the darkness of her storms.
When she cut her skin,
When she bled and again
Saw only horror in the mirror.
The scars it gave
The mirror didn't save
Any beauty to behold,
But it foretold
Of all the scars
So many scars

She pretended to be happy
Smiling ya'll and laughing.
It was almost sappy
But we loved her without the doll parts
Because she was genuine in the exchange
Of her heart's
Beauty ablaze
and longing to be loved
To be held in her own gaze
and to be loved...

Maypop

Medicine for passion

Mesmerized by beauty
The shocking pop underfoot
Of the apricot vine.
Aid of Restlessness,
Euphoric plant,
Illness fears you.
Complex beauty
With simple needs for a home—
Roadside, fields, gardens, trails.
Magnet to all pollinators.

Seventeen | Blackberry Winter Whistlin' Tune

PLAYING THE POKE SALLET FESTIVAL in a professional band was never one of my big dreams, nor an event I ever considered before. We were booked to play it, and that would be Lucie's final show with us before returning home.

Leading up to the festival, she spent more time with us, and even asked to join me and Kevin on one of our "song writing field trips," as everyone in the band was calling them now.

Lucie said, "I didn't see very many of these types of places you talk about. I was in the city most of the time I've been here."

We were going out to the mounds, built by pre-tribal indigenous people in middle Tennessee. Ma Zona wrote about their journey to mounds, but she didn't say exactly where they were, so we had to guess and pick one of the mound locations close to us.

Kevin hiked ahead of us, carrying a backpack, and giving us space to talk.

"Strange to believe my time here has passed so quickly," Lucie said, wiping sweat away from her forehead. "But the duration has been two years."

"Have you not been home since coming here?" I asked.

"Oh yeah," she said. "I've returned for the holidays."

"Do you get homesick?" I asked. We hiked down an old road, lined with trees and poison ivy and all of the lush undergrowth of Tennessee. Ferns and moss layered the wooded hillsides. "I would miss Tennessee if I ever left for that long," I said.

"Yes, sometimes, I miss my home very much," she nodded. "Lately, I'm ready to return and stay at home for a while." She smiled. Then, she asked, "You've never been somewhere to live except Tennessee?" We passed by a sunny spot in an area that had been cleared for a field long ago. Ironweed and nettles, blackberry brambles, and passion flower vines grew in a tangled mess on the edges.

"No, been here all my life. I want to stay, but maybe I don't know any better because I've never been anywhere else really."

Lucie pointed to the passion flowers that were open on a vine. "So pretty," she said. I nodded. We moved along down the old road through the forest.

We were quiet, listening to the birds, the wind picking up in the trees, and someone whistling. We heard it at the same time come floating up over the hill and looked at each other with wide eyes and smiles. It stopped. We kept walking and saw the open field in the distance at the bottom of the hill.

"What are your plans when you get back home?" I asked.

"I'll play music with my band and see what happens," she said. "Probably, I'll be in an office job for a European booking company."

"You'll book bands?" I asked. The whistling began again, and I was sure that it was Kevin as we neared the end of the trees and reached the field. He sat in the grass.

"I'll probably be booking kids programs and maybe some festivals, if I'm lucky," she said. "Here in America, I've been an intern on Music Row for that."

"I had no idea," I said.

"I try to be good at business," she laughed. "What about you, Robin? What will you do after graduation?"

"I'm not sure yet," I shrugged. "I applied for a couple of master's programs, but I won't hear back for a little while."

"You want to teach at a university?"

"Maybe," I shrugged.

"You could visit me in Czech Republic sometime," she said, smiling. "I would really like for you all to visit, but it's so expensive. If you can get there, you can stay with me and my family."

"That's so nice of you," I said. "That would be incredible."

"Actually," she said, "there are many bluegrass fans in Czech. You would be surprised."

"I wouldn't have ever guessed that," I said. "But I'm sorry that I know nothing about Czech."

"I've noticed that most Americans don't even know where it's located." She shrugged.

A wave of lethargy came over me, and I sat down beside Kevin, freeing my shoulders from my backpack. I listened to his whistling tune with my eyes closed. I couldn't match it with anything I knew. Lucie lay down in the grass in front of us, where it was still short. As the field stretched out toward a large mound, the grass was taller, becoming hay. The field was dotted with smaller mounds and ringed by bluffs along the river.

The sun was briefly concealed by clouds and Lucie shivered. The wind picked up. I noticed a thicket of blooming blackberries growing along the edge of the field.

"Why is it suddenly so cold?" Lucie asked.

"It's called blackberry winter," Kevin said. "And, it's blowing in right now."

"It will snow?" Lucie asked, sitting up.

Kevin laughed. "No, no, it's just a way that people describe how it gets cold when certain plants are blooming."

"I don't understand," she said.

Kevin tried about three different ways to explain it, and I wasn't sure if she completely understood or not. He listed off the other "winters" in the process, and asked for my help in naming them all—redbud winter, dogwood winter, locust winter, and blackberry winter. He thought there was another one, but I could only think of four. Lucie called it "superstition" once, and so I thought that we didn't exactly get the point across. They simply signify "when the weather will have a cold spell," as Miss Emy described it.

Lucie stood and brushed off her clothes. "Do we have permission to go onto the mound?" she asked.

"Yeah, we can walk on it, as far as I know," I said.

"It's not a burial?" she asked.

"No, not this one," Kevin said, standing and reaching a hand down to help me up. "Maybe it was for their religious views or just some place where they met. No one is buried in this mound."

We walked toward the mound and Kevin started his whistling tune up again. I added my own section and whistled with him. A couple of turkey vultures turned circles and rode the air currents over the field. On the top of the mound, we continued to whistle while Lucie sang.

Blackberry Winter Whistlin' Tune
Lyrics by Lucie Novotná

Blackberry winter come early
And it's hot, so hot, under the blankets
in the wintertime
You've got me seeing a mirage
Of flowers blooming in the wintertime.
White petals bright as snow
Promising the sweetness of summer
Glow along the path
Tasting that sweetness of summer
Early in the wintertime.
Craving the summer in the wintertime.
Giving me that sweetness of blackberries
Early, so early, in the wintertime...

The Poke Sallet Festival was more enjoyable as a musician than when I was a teenage pageant contestant. Friends and family stopped by to listen. We picked up some new groupies, though Angie told me I had to stop calling people that because we weren't a hair band from the eighties. "People like to belong," I said. "Even as informal members of my our groupies."

"I don't know about that," she countered, but as if on cue, a couple, regulars from Love's Rest, came over to the booth where we were signing albums.

"Great show," the woman said. "We're so glad you told us, well, your fans," she blushed, "about this festival. We moved here last year from Colorado, and we hadn't heard about it until you announced it at Love's."

"Yeah, I recognize you from there," I said. "I'm so glad you like it. Thanks for coming out."

"We want to bring my sister when she visits with her family next year," she said, nodding to her friend. "This is just perfect because it's unique to this place. I never knew so much about poke sallet. Actually," she laughed, "before your band, I don't think I'd ever heard of it."

"How'd you hear about our band in the first place?" Kevin asked. "I'm just curious."

"We happened to be there one Saturday when you played."

"At Love's?" Angie asked, nodding.

"Yeah," she said. "We liked your music right away. And Robin's always funny, so that's a plus. We kept coming back. It's been about a year now, I guess."

Martin said, "Wow. Thanks for being fans." We signed their album.

More people approached and asked questions of Kevin and Lucie.

"This one's for my sister," one fan said, holding out a CD to purchase. "Her name is Lisa." We looked at the crowd that was edging along the line of booths and moving toward ours.

"We've already got one signed by all of you," a man said, standing with his arm around his wife. At this news, Martin clapped and shook his hand.

"See you back at Love's," the man said, and they headed for the other booths.

~ ~ ~

Twenty years from our first adventure, we drove out an old road for our last, where the field by the river was farmed for hundreds of years. The rains rutted out the roads, and that slowed us down. We wound along the bluffs above a snaky river in Delores's car. She steered us over the rocks and nearly got us stuck, but we went on around to another bend.

"We can stop here," I explained and pointed to a spot to pull off to the side in a square of overgrown grass where it was mostly level. "While this isn't the way we're supposed to enter it, I think we should leave the car here and just go ahead on foot." I pointed through the forest edge.

"Which way is the mound supposed to be?" Ida asked.

"You can get to it anywhere along this stretch of the river." We were still above the river, but could see it peeking here and there below us.

"Let's go," Cardy said and led the way along the path through the saw briar and Spanish needles. After a little patch of cane growth near the river's edge, we emerged into a wide open stretch and a great mound rose up toward the center of the field.

"Y'all, I've noticed something I've been writing for these many years now," Cardy said. "History always tells the story of the men, how they make history by

going places. History never tells the story of the women who protect places in our own ways, too. They don't talk about our sisterhoods, our prayers, our songs, our fights, our medicines, our blessings."

Ida picked the burrs, seeds, and plant needles from her dress skirt. She twirled them in her fingertips.

As we passed through the fields, moving by other smaller mounds, we found ourselves recalling all the places we have been in this journey. We laughed about Cardy's huntsman and the miner. She cried when remembering how close she came to leaving A.J. and the hurt that her relationships have caused her over the years.

Ida didn't say a word. She listened. She sniffled when we talked about the bliss that we felt at the mushroom rock and the sudden tragedy afterward when Delores almost died.

"I didn't die!" Delores said. "But I sure am glad not to be riding a train or a horse everywhere."

"It has changed from the days of riding," I said. "Not so hard on us now, but I still miss those days."

"I feel complete now," Delores said. "I enjoy these visits, but I certainly relish the thoughts of traveling with Dr. Landry, just the two of us, without a quest to fulfill." She sighed as if she were ready to go now.

"Maybe our mothers are satisfied with us and what they asked us to do. They'll be sending us blessings from the ancestors," Cardy said.

When we reached the foot of the mound, Ida said, "Those are watermelon plants." Young watermelons ringed the base of the mound all the way around. We walked over them and up to the top, where young corn grew in rows. Cardy hummed and Delores joined her.

Ida whistled something I never heard before. We hummed and whistled, and we could see the whole river valley from there.

Our quest didn't feel complete, but it was finished for us. We didn't know how it would continue, or pass on to the future, and we understood that we might never know what happened in the places where we went to consecrate a sacred protection.

~ ~ ~

All these stories intertwined. My life had layers that I never thought would be possible, and realizing that changed me. I felt myself seeing and tasting differently. I saw myself in other people and these strangers were part of me. That made songwriting evolve. If Ma Zona could pull a song out of the future for me and Kevin, from me and Kevin, I could move through music, too, see and feel it on the wind as Cardy had, hear it threaded through nature and pierced into our hearts as Ida and Delores had.

All the Stories
Lyrics by Robin Ballard

If you could mess around
and let your brain go,
defenses down,
let your senses flow,
You could see the stories
That'll reveal their glories.
All the regular people with messy lives
And the fakey wives

Telling tales in the kitchen
To anyone who'll listen.
It's all there
Floating along in the air
To pluck with fingers on strings
And find a few words to sing.
You know these tales
And these people,
The lies and the dreams,
All the scenes they figure in between

You know Charles and his tall tales.
All his six-figure sales,
How he knows all the big dogs,
All the heroes
From the game shows,
And he's smoked every Cuban log
With the big dogs.
The big dogs.
You know, he's the name-dropper,
The game shopper
Wheelin' and dealin'
Not caring how his family is feelin'.

You know, Lynn, she's pretending
To be the least offending.
Everyone's friend and pick me.
She can lend you a ride for free
As long as you pick me.
Pick me.

You know, sister Rae,
Man, she can slay

The guitar and make the strings cry.
Sings the sweetest lullabies.
She got that voice that's taking her far,
We done pegged her as our brightest star

Aw, you know, my brother.
He's a scholar and a nice guy.
He'll give it an honest effort, honest try,
Working hard to make the family proud,
He'll stick around and lead the crowd.

You know, Kay, she cheated to get it all
The heated pool, the ponies, the white wall,
But she can't sleep at night
And pops pills to keep out the light.
They make her stomach ache
And now she can't eat, can't take
Anything but scotch and scotch.
Sometimes it's hard to watch
When people destroy their lives
But they keep right on going.
They are their own demise
That leads right into ending...

Tomato

Medicine for eating from your home ground, enjoying variety and the fruits of success

This one overlooked.
This one desperate to drop.
This one split.
Oh, that sticky vegetation,
Fingers feeling forward, forever on the move.
Climbers, all. Tumbling over themselves.
Dainty yellow flowering around the bend.
This one plump and sweet.
This one tangy. Acidic. Crunchy little
Cherries. Clustered. A smooth swell under the
Prickles.
Green for days.
Absorbing heat to purple.
This one frying.
Waiting for the success of a perforated knife to
Slice through a ripe one. The main
Attraction,
A sauce simmers
Red fruit,
Lures.

Eighteen | Recipe for a Song

THE KETTLE'S WHISTLING, as Cora would have said with a nod to do something about it. When I was growing up and visiting Aunt Melinda, Sylvan Park in West Nashville was a neighborhood for factory workers from the glass plant, the cigar company, the packaging companies, a trucker refueling station, and a long time ago, even the old prison that's gotten so famous now. I loved the sounds, so different from growing up in Granville—the city's murmuring of working families outside their homes, yard work and ball games, grilling and carpentry, people milling around.

Aunt Melinda asked me to move in, since the house was empty a lot, with her often staying with Gordon. They decided that they didn't want to live together. Finally, I was going to have the home I always wanted and belong there as I imagined that I already did.

I went to Miss Emy's to get some of my things from my old bedroom.

"You're going to need to sit down," Cora said, *opening the door and scurrying behind me with tea on the table already.*

"Good Lord," I said and patted her on the back. She *hugged into me and squeezed, resting her head on my*

shoulder for an instant. She took in a deep breath. It was one that signaled relief. Then, she started talking and going on and on about something.

"What's got into you?" I interrupted her. "I can't even drink my tea I'm so shocked by how you're talking so fast."

"I guess I'm excited by it all," she said. "You're moving in here and opening the tea place with Melinda."

"What tea place?" I asked.

"Stop messing," she waved her hand and poured more tea into her cup from the pot.

"Cora made the decision," Aunt Melinda was saying in my dream when I woke up.

That morning, Miss Emy sat on a chair in the kitchen doorway and fanned a bowl of cobbler that she held perched on her thigh. The steam rolled in the light from the window. She was tiny and her white hair caught the light. It was cropped, just under her earlobes, and that made it seem thicker. Her eyes seemed to fill her whole face sometimes.

"Good morning," she said. "You sleep alright?"

"Yeah, fine," I said. "You eating cobbler?"

"Good a time as any," Miss Emy said. "Get you some, too." She watched me with an amused expression as I went into the kitchen for my own bowl.

"Seems like you've been up a while," I said.

"Told you, don't sleep well anymore," she said. "I've been thinking about it this morning, and I've got to know about this plan of Melinda's. Tell me about it." She grinned at me as I sat down at the dining room table. "Oh, first, we need some ice cream. That'll cool this down." She hurried into the kitchen. I admired how adorable Miss Emy was. She wore a thick navy blue summer dress with tiny red birds stitched into the fabric.

I took a bite of the cobbler, passing on the ice cream. "What's this spice you used in here?" I asked. "There's a little pop in this cobbler."

"You like it?" she asked, chuckling. She returned to her previous position with a scoop of ice cream added to the bowl of cobbler. "It was an accident," she said. "What do you think it is?"

I looked into the remains of my cobbler and began to pick it apart with my spoon. *I see something green*, I thought. *Maybe it's purple.* I held my nose close and inhaled the fragrance. "Is this basil?" I asked and took a nibble. "Well, that's different."

She nodded. "Tell me about Melinda's plan," she said, and she took a big bite from her spoon that was heaped with both cobbler and ice cream. She motioned for me to start talking. I shook my head at my own bowl and at her, and then I began to tell her.

Aunt Melinda brought the deal to me. She told me about Gordon's plan to create a teahouse with her, in that old restaurant, the one that Aunt Cora said she went to.

Other than knocking out a wall or two and building a deck, installing an industrial oven and huge freezers, a freezer room in the basement, and I couldn't even remember what all after a while, it was a beautiful place. Miss Emy laughed at that. They brought me in as a planner and a manager, offered the band a place to play, and Gordon had succeeded in putting me to work. That made me chuckle as it would have tickled Cora.

We even planted a garden out back and set out some tables among the rose bushes, a stand of tomatoes, kale, and cucumbers. The zinnias kept a host of butterflies moving. I filled a notebook with our plans, bulging more each week, until it became multiple notebooks and filing cabinets. We grew, as did the staff, menu, and Melinda and Gordon's plans.

Ripe Tea & Treats offered a full lunch menu with high tea, and every table in our interior started to fill through the week. We added a little breakfast menu and a couple of patio seats. The garden opened, and we added an early dinner menu. Aunt Melinda and I spent more time setting up and working at the tea shop than working on anything else some weeks.

"Those days with Cora—some of the sweetest of my life," she said reminiscing. "Remember when she made those scone-iscuits. And now this is happening."

Cora looked down from her seat next to the window where her picture hung on the wall. People milled around talking and asking questions about food and herbs, tea and desserts. They were taking Nenny's Dandelion Fritters home to share with friends and family, and I imagined that maybe they hid a few somewhere and enjoyed them completely alone. They brewed Nashville's Backyard Violet Tea. I loved Zona's Fried Green Tomato Poppers.

We created a whole Tribute to Tennessee's Fruit, the Tomato. That little menu included Hoot's Tomato Hangover Breakfast, TNT (Tomatoes 'N Toast), Tennessee Farm BLT, Simply Tomato Salad, Seared Tomato & Cheese Toasty, Fried Green Tomato Stack, and we rotated in new items. I liked the tomato menu because it emphasized a plant that most people wouldn't associate with a teahouse. I packed in our little patio garden with heirloom tomato plants.

Aunt Melinda and I did our fair share of hustling, serving tea, blending, planning, posting to social media, doing interviews, and life at times felt like an endless promotion. There were days when both Aunt Melinda and I were angry about the amount of work it required, snapping at each other. Eventually, we worked all disagreements out, and we sat down together and assessed whether we could hire people to do the things that we both detested or didn't have the skills to adequately complete.

Flowers and herbs have that captivating quality, especially when you work with them. They will pull you into their kaleidoscopic and sensational experience. The sensory enrapturing of plants is mesmerizing, and I found myself deep in the spells of them, not caring about boyfriends and friendships. I had tasted it, and I wanted success and to play with the power of plants, to offer that medicine and interaction to other people.

I heard someone approaching. "Mind if I sit down?" Kevin asked, as I turned to acknowledge whoever was walking to the patio.

"Please, do," I said. "How's it going?"

"Alright," he said, adjusting his hat nervously. "I wanted to talk about us going forward. The band, I mean, going back out on the road some. We're sitting on an offer to play some pretty big venues, and we need to decide if we can do it. Me and you."

"Well, our band is tight from all the playing we're doing here," I said.

"Right," he said. "It's just that we haven't made any plans, and I think that it's time we did. Are we going out to San Francisco for that festival?"

He gazed into my eyes. I recalled how long he had tried to get a band going and then how long it took to record an album.

"Okay," I agreed. "This is a good opportunity. I'll find a way to break away from here."

"Alright, I'll get it booked," he said, smiling. "It'll be great."

"I hope so."

"It will." He reached out and squeezed my hand. "By the way, I like that tomato menu," he said. "I came by yesterday and ate a TNT, but they said you had the day off. I like all those different kinds of tomatoes that y'all put in there."

"Yeah, I've been working a lot," I said. We were playing music together, but I had been avoiding any dates with Kevin lately even though he called and asked me twice. I was honestly absorbed in this business, but my heart pulled at me. I momentarily thought about asking him to do something, but I hesitated. "I'm glad to hear that you like the menu."

"Tomatoes," he said, snapping his fingers. "Are they in your great-grandma's book?" he asked, taking off his cap and rounding the bill of it.

"Yeah, actually they are," I said.

"Well, what's the tomato's spell?" he asked, putting his cap back on his head.

"Would you believe that its medicine is for the fruits of success?" I asked.

He looked around, nodding. "Did you ever go look for where she thought the other treasure or whatever was buried?" he asked.

"Nah. I got distracted with all this, but Miss Emy told me last week that they might develop that part behind her where Ma Zona was thinking it could be buried."

"If you decide to look again, I'd be willing to help you," he said. "Truth be told, I've always wanted to go out there and see the place that inspired you to sing, and us to form a band."

"Alright," I said. "I might take you up on that this weekend." He grinned.

That evening, I opened the songwriting journals, all those notebooks, thinking about going to the Ballard Farm. I chuckled when I ran across that folded paper with the map inside. That all felt so far away from me. I didn't recognize those former dreams of finding a treasure, of becoming a famous singer, of making fame the center of my goals.

I was in a new dream, blending and serving the recipes of my family, and it hardly felt real. Yet, the reality was there, nudging at me. I still wanted more.

I turned the pages, pen in hand, ready to write down new lyrics to match my thoughts. The doorbell rang, and my guitar slid onto the floor along with the rest of the notebooks. I stepped over the mess, and when I got to the living room, Aunt Melinda was already there saying it was a neighbor.

Back in my bedroom, I placed the guitar on the stand and sat on the floor, assembling all the journals—mine, Hoot's, and Zona's. Papers scattered and trailed under the bed skirt. I stacked them up and noticed what looked to be envelopes poking from the back of a book. The thick paper attached to the cover was torn at the edge and along the side, revealing the corners of the envelopes. I pressed on the page that is usually glued to the cover, and it squished, as if it were stuffed with something. I picked at the edge of the page and it tore away. More of the envelopes showed, and I ripped the paper away from the cover to get at them. I fanned them out in my hands. There were five letters addressed to Cora Ballard from Harold Flynn.

~ ~ ~

Recipe for a Song
Lyrics by Robin Ballard and Kevin Crenshaw

I was sitting outside
Away from everyone.
I had lost someone close to me.
I didn't want perfect. Didn't want to rhyme.
Only needing a friend
In the quiet without
Expectations.
Then, you were there,
A dash of shoulder for my head
To lean on.
A touch of your hand,
A sprinkle of your smile,
A drop of my tears.
You reflect the colors of flowers.
There was that splash of sunset
Melting.

The moment was
Soothing.
You added an armful
Of understanding
By listening with me to the
Harmony of quiet.
The quiet.
You and me.
We reflect the colors of flowers.
I pinched the clover
As we swayed lightly.
The clouds wafted over the deepening sky.
The geese, the mourning doves, the fireflies.
That big splash of moonlight
Came up and we sighed together.
Together.
A touch of your hand,
A sprinkle of your smile,
A drop of my tears,
There was that splash
of stars above us.
It didn't have to be perfect.
We didn't want to rhyme.
We both just needed a friend...

Pokeweed

Medicine for creativity

Secret Queen of the medicine wheel.
A royal garment berry.
A treasured green.
A shoot of nourishment.
Available. Advisor. Anchored.
A flock of couriers advancing
Her talents. The stain of art.
Woe to the too-swift approach,
No direct partaking allowed,
For the Queen will have her choice
Of ground over all manner
Of lovers. Hearken back
To the Garden Goddess,
The Beloved, to cherish.

The Album | RIPE FOR THE PICKIN'
POKE SALLET QUEEN & THE FAMILY MEDICINE WHEEL

SONGS
Opening Act
Guitar and Vocals—ROBIN BALLARD, Fiddle—KEVIN CRENSHAW, Fiddle—ANGIE SPARKS, Bass—MARTIN PAXTON, Lyrics by ROBIN BALLARD

Backyard Spring
Guitar and Vocals—ROBIN BALLARD, Fiddle and Vocals—KEVIN CRENSHAW, Fiddle and Vocals—ANGIE SPARKS, Bass and Vocals—MARTIN PAXTON, Lyrics by ROBIN BALLARD & KEVIN CRENSHAW

Sisters Sewing
Mandolin and Vocals—ROBIN BALLARD, Fiddle and Vocals— ANGIE SPARKS, Bass—MARTIN PAXTON, Banjo and Vocals— LUCIE NOVOTNÁ, Lyrics by ROBIN BALLARD

Full Circle Gospel
Dulcimer and Vocals—ROBIN BALLARD, Fiddle and Vocals— KEVIN CRENSHAW, Fiddle and Vocals—ANGIE SPARKS, Bass and Vocals—MARTIN PAXTON, Banjo and Vocals—LUCIE NOVOTNÁ, Lyrics by ROBIN BALLARD & MARTIN PAXTON

Family Medicine Wheel Breakdown
Mandolin and Vocals—ROBIN BALLARD, Fiddle and Vocals— KEVIN CRENSHAW, Fiddle and Vocals—ANGIE SPARKS, Bass and Vocals—MARTIN PAXTON, Banjo and Vocals—LUCIE NOVOTNÁ, Lyrics by KEVIN CRENSHAW, ROBIN BALLARD, & MARTIN PAXTON

Cowbird Blues
Guitar and Vocals—ROBIN BALLARD, Fiddle and Harmonica— KEVIN CRENSHAW, Fiddle—ANGIE SPARKS, Bass—MARTIN PAXTON, Lyrics by ROBIN BALLARD & KEVIN CRENSHAW

A Little Bit of Whiskey with my Hist'ry
Fiddle and Vocals—KEVIN CRENSHAW, Guitar—ROBIN BALLARD, Fiddle—ANGIE SPARKS, Bass—MARTIN PAXTON,

Banjo—LUCIE NOVOTNÁ, Lyrics by GORDON BELL and ROBIN BALLARD

Nary a One
Guitar and Vocals—ROBIN BALLARD, Fiddle and Vocals—KEVIN CRENSHAW, Lyrics by ROBIN BALLARD & KEVIN CRENSHAW

One Long Song
Guitar, Mandolin, and Vocals—ROBIN BALLARD, Fiddle and Vocals—KEVIN CRENSHAW, Fiddle—ANGIE SPARKS, Bass— MARTIN PAXTON, Lyrics by KEVIN CRENSHAW & ROBIN BALLARD

Ol' Time Tales
Dulcimer and Vocals—ROBIN BALLARD, Fiddle and Vocals— KEVIN CRENSHAW, Fiddle—ANGIE SPARKS, Bass— MARTIN PAXTON, Banjo—LUCIE NOVOTNÁ, Lyrics by ROBIN BALLARD

The Devil Cried
Guitar and Vocals—ROBIN BALLARD, Fiddle—KEVIN CRENSHAW, Bass and Vocals—MARTIN PAXTON, Banjo—LUCIE NOVOTNÁ, Lyrics by ROBIN BALLARD

Recipe for a Song
Guitar and Vocals—ROBIN BALLARD, Fiddle and Vocals—KEVIN CRENSHAW, Lyrics by ROBIN BALLARD & KEVIN CRENSHAW

Blackberry Winter Whistlin' Tune
Vocals—LUCIE NOVOTNÁ, Whistling—ROBIN BALLARD, Whistling—KEVIN CRENSHAW, Bass—MARTIN PAXTON, Whistling Arrangement by KEVIN CRENSHAW, Lyrics by LUCIE NOVOTNÁ

© Copyright 2005 NARROW RIVER MUSIC, Inc.
Producer—STEVE COOK, Engineer—LEE NELSON,
Arranger—CONNOR LYLE, Photography—TAYLOR OWENS
Art Direction—ANNIE KESSLER
RECORDED AT HARPETH STUDIOS,
     NASHVILLE, TN. 2005

ACKNOWLEDGMENTS

POKEWEED GROWS FREELY in our garden, and I welcome it every year. The garden inspires me to write daily and shows up in my writings almost ritualistically, whether that is in my journals or on my social media posts. I express my thankfulness to the garden for all of its delights (vegetables and honeybees, for example) and nuisances ("weeds" and mosquitoes). It hosts many visitors, from indigo buntings to rabbits, and I am eager to use what we grow in meals and drinks, snacks and treats, or simply to plop in my mouth as I pass through. For all of these reasons and more, the garden's variety of flavors, colors, fragrances, and forms drives me to write about plants. Thank you to everyone who has shared time and appreciation with me in the garden.

This book is a work of fiction. All stories within this book are fictional and have been altered in fictional ways.

Sabrina Brazle, Thank you for being an inspirational muse for this series.

My Nana, Jean Thornton Dennis, has a beautiful home and a lovely garden—constants in my life. I saw my first walking stick insect while sitting in her apple trees. We snapped green beans on her porch. Families and June bugs gathered under the fruit trees. Life was swarming at your house, and it still is. Thank you for making a beautiful home for our family and for always keeping it updated and changing with the times.

Rita Yerrington, you, me, and the garden go way back—this book wouldn't be the same without your advice, and I wouldn't be the same without your friendship. Thank you for being by my side.

To the friends who have journeyed to sacred places with me or talked with me about them, thank you, Debbie Harris, Jennie Passero, and Lisa Sims.

Thank you to my daughters for all of our adventures to do research. It might have been itchy and sweaty, but, Zoe, I appreciate that you hiked out to so many places and never disappointed us with a lack of sarcasm.

Silvia, No one comes up with better character names. Thank you for helping me to create some unforgettable ones, sure to show up again.

To all the fans of *Poke Sallet Queen & the Family Medicine Wheel*, thank you for continually asking for a sequel. My mom led your cause.

I'm thankful for your positive presence, Dad, and your ability to identify trees.

Mom, I will always need you to be the biggest fan of my writing and this series.

To my friends and editors, Kitty Madden and Beverly Fisher, thank you for being meticulous, encouraging, and clever. I'm grateful for your unwavering support.

Writing takes so much time, and I couldn't manage it as well without my husband, Terry Morris. Thank you for filling in, running errands, reminding me not to worry, feeding me, talking about my books to all who will listen, loving me, and making me laugh.

To the ancestors who believe in the stories and storytellers, thank you for reaching me.

ABOUT THE AUTHOR

SHANA THORNTON is the author of three novels, *Ripe for the Pickin'* (2022), *Poke Sallet Queen and the Family Medicine Wheel* (2015), and *Multiple Exposure* (2012), and the young adult book, *The Adventures to Pawnassus* (2019). She is the co-author of the nonfiction self-help book, *Seasons of Balance: On Creativity and Mindfulness* (2016). Shana is a series editor for the BreatheYourOMBalance® book series.
She is the Founder of the Clarksville Montgomery County African American Legacy Trail (2019) and the President of the Friends of Dunbar Cave, Inc.
Follow her on Twitter @shanathornton and find her on Instagram as @shana_thornton

For information about authors, books, upcoming reading events, new titles, and more, visit http://www.thorncraftpublishing.com
Like Thorncraft Publishing on Facebook.
Find Thorncraft Publishing on Twitter as @ThorncraftBooks
On Instagram as @thorncraftpublishing

Ripe for the Pickin'